Martini Club 4:
The 1920s: Runaway
The 1940s: Priceless

by

Krysta Scott

Martini Club 4: Runaway and Priceless

COPYRIGHT © 2021 by Krysta Scott

Cover Art by *Lisa Dawn MacDonald*

The Wild Rose Press, Inc.
PO Box 708
Adams Basin, NY 14410-0708
Visit us at www.thewildrosepress.com

Publishing History
First Edition, 2021
Trade Paperback ISBN 978-1-5092-3730-2
Digital ISBN 978-1-5092-3731-9

Martini Club 4: Runaway and Priceless
Published in the United States of America

RUNAWAY…

"You…You…" Her throat closed. The rest of her diatribe wouldn't budge.

He winked. His thin hair slicked back in the latest fashion exaggerated the gaunt cheekbones and sunken eyes tinging him with an unhealthy, dilapidated look. He gulped the whiskey. A bit of the amber liquid escaped through the gap in his teeth and down his chin. Her stomach lurched.

"Thank you, sweet cakes. Put it on my tab." He skulked off.

Charli whirled around. How did the bounder get past Tiny? She sighed and rolled her eyes to the heavens. The customer was always right. Even when they were wrong.

PRICELESS…

This was even better than she'd planned. She was going to get set the sky on fire…

He stood behind her much closer than she liked and guided her hand to the fuse. "Ok, the minute you light the fuse step back."

"Mr. Stanhope and Miss Noble, what on earth do you think you're doing?"

Sophie froze mid-flick. Caught in the act by Professor Critchton. What had made her think she could get away with such a fete? To make matters worse, Peter was draped over her in a most unbecoming fashion. Heat flooded her cheeks. She dropped the lighter and straightened abruptly, knocking her head into Peter's chin.

The Martini Club 4 series consists of a total of eight stories by four different authors. They are intertwined and take place somewhat simultaneously, but they are best read in the following order:

Martini Club 4: The 1920s Stories:

Rebellious by Amanda McCabe
Ruined by Alicia Dean
Reckless by Kathy L Wheeler
Runaway by Krysta Scott

Martini Club 4: The 1940s Stories:

Pampered by Kathy L Wheeler
Priceless by Krysta Scott
Perilous by Amanda McCabe
Precarious by Alicia Dean

We hope you enjoy!

Dedication

For Mom, Scott, Taylor, Isabelle, and Phyllis.
Thank you for always believing in me.

Acknowledgments

The first time I heard about the Martini Lounge I imagined many colored liquors backlit by neon lights. Inspired, I suppose, by my love of science fiction. It wasn't anything like that. It was better. For years my friends and I have been meeting once a week to commiserate about our writing lives, plan writing retreats, and discuss our professional goals. At some point, and no one really remembers how it happened, we decided to write stories about the prohibition era. A scary thing for me because I don't usually write historical stories and, unlike my Martini Club cohorts, had not yet published anything. But with their encouragement that felt like a cattle prod at times, Runaway was born. Thank you, Alicia Dean, Amanda McCabe, and Kathy L Wheeler. I honestly couldn't have done this without your help and guidance. I would also like to thank Brooke Taylor, our honorary member, for her feedback and J. Lynn McKay for assisting with my editing.

Martini Club 4: The 1920s

Runaway

Chapter One

New York City, 1924

Grimly, Detective Felix Noble glanced from the dead woman lying in the filthy alley to the small crowd gathered around. A slender, ivory-skinned woman with reddish-blonde hair caught his attention. Her horrified expression and delicate frame elicited a strange urge to take her in his arms and offer comfort. Ridiculous. He was on the job, and he didn't even know the dame. He forced his attention back to the victim. Jaw tight, he squatted next to her. The skimpy clothing and thick make-up indicated she might be a tart. The strangulation marks on her throat suggested she'd pissed off the wrong person.

It was too much to hope he'd have enough evidence to solve this one. His last two cases had gone unsolved, and the department was losing faith in him. But even worse, every time he failed, he disappointed his mentor.

"I'll find your killer," he whispered. "I swear." He hoped he could keep his promise but knew in his heart he most likely couldn't.

****

Lady Charlotte Leighton squeezed through the tightly packed tables at Club 501, swaying to Alyce Kutcher's music. The woman commanded the luxurious speakeasy as her sexy voice drifted from the stage, augmented by the trumpet's clear notes. Charli, far from her English roots, placed drinks in front of enthusiastically clapping patrons, wide grins and flushed faces indicating how enthralled they were with the songstress. As pleasant as the sound was, Alyce could never top Meggie. Her voice wasn't near as warm. It was more strident. Imperious. Meggie—Lady Margaret as she was becoming known throughout NYC—was one of Charli's three housemates. All three had adjusted better to America than Charli. Meggie found her niche singing, Jessie landed a prime position at the *New York World*, and Eliza lucked into a posh position as party hostess, while Charli still floundered like a fish out of water. Since disembarking from the *Empress of India* six months ago, her friends had been scads more successful at accomplishing their dreams than she.

The patrons' foot stomps and flinging arms beat in a lively response to the music. Silver shoes partnered with black spats bounced through the Charleston. Flashes of brilliant blue, green, red, and orange sparkled off fringed gowns.

Charli's throat tightened. Too loud. Too bright. Too crowded. She hated crowds. All that body heat, sweat, and nudging. But at least staying busy kept her mind off the poor girl who'd been found murdered. Who would have done such a thing? And so close to the club…

She banished the image from her mind. Dwelling on the tragedy would help no one. Sucking in her stomach, she pushed through a narrow opening between tables, balancing a tray of drinks, careful not to spill the contents. It was one of the speakeasy rules: spill a drink, pay the tab. And she couldn't possibly afford that.

For now, she was a common drudge. A waitress. Invisible but always present. Wasn't that the story of her life? She hadn't run away from an impending forced marriage to Geoffrey Hare, only to become a waitress. However, Mrs. Greensley's Finishing school failed in offering her *practical* skills. Charli let out a dejected sigh. With no other skills, cocktail waitress seemed the best steppingstone for her ambitions.

Ah, how she missed her morning chocolate lying abed; the long constitutionals in the quiet gardens of her family homestead in England; reading for hours on end in the parlor then sneaking downstairs to assist the cook, Mrs. Erickson. She would have stayed there forever but for her meddling parents despairing over their reclusive daughter. Charli could barely bring herself to communicate with the opposite sex. She had *no* desire to marry. Instead of honoring her wishes, they'd contracted her to a stranger. *With your temperament, how will you ever make a match on your own?* The memory of her mother's harsh words stung even now though Charli was safely ensconced across the pond.

"Hey, Charli." A man with ruddy cheeks and mussed brown hair smacked her on the bum. The burn radiated up her left hip, and heat flooded her face. She was self-conscious enough in the uniform—a cream-colored satin apron over a short burgundy dress with sheer voile skirt from hem to the tops of her high heels—without these bounders putting their hands on her. Unfortunately, pawing came with the position.

Gripping the tray on her shoulder, she offered a weak smile.

"Get me another gin will ya, doll?"

"Right away, sir." She couldn't remember the regular's name. That was the problem with this place. Too many faces. How could she possibly keep track of them all? She skirted between two seats, lifting her tray of precious, illegal cargo above their heads. Club 501, the most glamorous speakeasy in New York City, served only liquor imported from Europe. No cheap backwoods booze here.

Laughter bounded off every corner of the dimly lit room. The Bernie-Edison Orchestra performed, each pounding note a hammer to her head. The mob beat on the tabletops in melodic time. Even her own footsteps grabbed the annoying rhythm.

On each pass to another table, she was nudged, groped, fairly accosted. Everyone living the high life but her. She approached a table where a brassy blonde with curls plastered against her head leaned into the man at her side. He draped an arm around her and whispered into her ear. The woman tittered. Charli lowered a glass in front of him, heat flooding her cheeks. Such overt displays were unseemly. His fingers curled around the glass, but his gaze never left his date. Bah! Americans.

"Um, sir, that will be one pound—I mean dollar."

He looked up grudgingly and dug in his pocket for the cash.

She snatched it up and picked her way back to the bar. Rubbing her temples, Charli readied for the reload. Two more hours until she could bake again. She slammed the tray on the counter and blew out an aggravated breath.

"Tough night, Charli?"

She looked up to find Dollie Carter at the bar. The petite woman, dressed in a form fitting suit revealing curves Charli would never possess, soft brown hair folded neatly beneath a rounded hat, pulled her kid gloves off, fingertip by fingertip. She sat straight-backed on the barstool. Completely at ease in this atmosphere.

"Mrs. Carter," Charli choked out. Now this was one regular Charli did keep track of. The successful department store owner liked her whiskey neat. "Your usual?"

Charli stepped behind the bar and pulled a bottle from underneath and poured her customer a shot. Mrs. Carter tossed it back. Like a practiced man.

Charli glanced over at Ira. The bartender was engaged in conversation with another customer. It would be a few minutes before he filled her tray. Might as well put the time to good use and get some tips on opening her own business. Her flatmates were always telling her she had to make opportunities for herself just like Jess had secured herself a job at the *World*, even though they had thought she was a man. Charli grabbed a cloth and wiped the countertop. Without making eye contact with Mrs. Carter she said, "How is business?"

"Good." She slid her glass to Charli. Once it had been refilled, she drained it as quickly as the first one. "I'm thinking of expanding."

"Really?" Charli poured another swig, heart thudding. "Expansion?"

This time she took small, feminine sips. "Not certain. A café perhaps."

"That serves food?" The words spilled out before she could stop them. She bit her lip. Mrs. Carter would think her a ninny like everyone else. Donning her most businesslike expression, she studied the older woman. Mrs. Carter leveled a shrewd gaze on her. Her deep brown eyes held curiosity.

"Is there any other kind?" she said dryly.

Charli's cheeks heated, and she moved her hand swiftly over the deep cherry-wood. "It sounds exciting."

"It won't be large." Mrs. Carter focused on a distant point. "I envision something in the center of the store."

This was her chance. *A bakery? A bakery would be lovely.*

"Charli." Ira's rough voice carried through the cacophony from the other side of the bar. Charli stiffened and faced his direction. He sauntered over and leaned against the counter's edge, mouth set in a disapproving grimace. "Are ya a dewdropper, Brit? Table nine is waiting."

"Indeed." She lifted the newly filled tray, and with an apologetic smile to Mrs. Carter, wove through the throng.

Ira's voice floated after her. "Don't mind her."

She glanced back over her shoulder. His wide wolf grin had grabbed Mrs. Carter's attention. Any chance to make a good impression faded in the dazzling glow of Ira's scorn.

"For a mouse she can be such a busybody. Head's always filled with zany ideas. She wanted me to serve *scones.*" He barked out a laugh. "Imagine *scones* in a drinking establishment."

The weight on her shoulders dipped. She saved the load and hurried through the crowd…well, as fast as the mob would allow. Would she never be taken seriously? *The land of opportunity.* Ha. More like Land of Excess and Squander. An elbow nudged her. A red-haired man adjusted his seat closer to a brazen brunette. The woman screeched a lilt of laughter and placed a hand on his shoulder. "Careful, Gustave." Her blue eyes flickered in Charli's direction. "With all the effort she's taking to serve the tables, you don't want to upset her tray, do ya, pet?"

Charli nodded and rushed past. The air was thick with the nauseating odor of sweat and libations. She took a breath but couldn't seem to fill her lungs. The weight of the tray burned a line of tension down her arm causing it to shake. Just a few more feet until she could empty her tray. *An eternity.* If she could get back fast enough, she could continue her conversation with Mrs. Carter. How many opportunities would she allow to pass?

Long, thin fingers curled around a glass and lifted it from the tray. Charli followed the direction of the drink. Derrick Chaunce, or as the local duffs referred to him, "Slick," grinned, exposing yellowed teeth.

"You…You…" Her throat closed. The rest of her diatribe wouldn't budge.

He winked. His thin hair slicked back in the latest fashion exaggerated the gaunt cheekbones and sunken eyes tinging him with an unhealthy, dilapidated look. He gulped the whiskey. A bit of the amber liquid escaped through the gap in his teeth and down his chin. Her stomach lurched.

"Thank you, sweet cakes. Put it on my tab." He skulked off.

Charli whirled around. How did the bounder get past Tiny? Ira fumed about customers who ran up a high tab without reconciling at the end of the night. Now she would have to explain yet another charge added to Slick's mounting debt. She sighed and rolled her eyes to the heavens. The customer was always right. Even when they were wrong.

Table twenty-six overflowed with eight people crushed around the small area. The top was littered with empty glasses. She replaced empty glasses with fresh drinks. By the time she reached customer eight, the tray had no drinks left thanks to Slick's sticky fingers.

Number eight's red eyes glowered.

"Pardon, sir." Her voice squeaked. "I'll have a fresh one to you straight away." She fled. The sooner she completed his order, the sooner he would forget her incompetence. Charli searched for Mrs. Carter on her way back to the bar, but the seat was empty. Gone. Another opportunity, *lost*. She blinked back tears. Would she never learn? She filled a glass with gin. Slick sidled up to the bar and reached for the glass, his lopsided grin grotesque against his sallow skin. A large hand gripped his wrist.

"What the hell do you think you're doing?" Ira glared at him. "You're cut off until you pay up."

"Awe, come on," Slick sniffed. "I'm good for it."

Ira leaned closer. "Tell that to Frank. You haven't paid your tab for three days."

Ira signaled the bouncer, Tiny, a bulky man with a balding pate and a lip curled in distaste. He nodded and made his way toward Slick. Slick's face crumpled into a pout. His eyes met Charli's, silently pleading with her. But what could she do? She shrugged and whisked the drink away to a paying customer. Even if she wanted to help the lout, Ira was the boss, and there was no contradicting *him*. The farther she moved away from the clash of wills, the easier she breathed. After delivering the drink, she snuck to the hallway that led to the ladies' room and leaned against the wall. Her feet throbbed. Just a short break before her next round, she promised. She glanced at her watch.

One more hour. The ache traveled up her legs. She sucked in a breath and squared her shoulders. She could walk through hell if she knew she would get out. One hour wasn't so bad, but how many more days would she have to endure before life truly began?

She had dreams. She'd stood on the deck of the *Empress of India* staring at Ellis Island, seeing her Liberty. Arms stretched wide, beckoning. Welcoming *her*. She'd seen the promise of a new beginning. It glinted off the Hudson River. But that silver chalice of freedom, once bright and shiny, was now dull and tarnished.

Chapter Two

Despite that meddling bartender's best efforts, Derrick managed to pilfer enough drinks to keep his spirits high. He staggered from Club 501, right into some well-dressed egg. "Scuse me, sir." His fingers rose to his hat but ended up grabbing a fist full of hair. "Sorry, lost my hat. Just wish I could remember where. After you." Derrick grabbed the exterior wall, extending his other arm to allow the man to pass.

The bastard had the gall to look down his holier-than-thou nose at Derrick but didn't move. The intense scrutiny pissed him off. "What?"

"Sir, I wonder if perhaps you might be of assistance." The fancy gent's voice was as stiff as his heavily starched shirt. It also sounded remarkably similar to Charli's. The precise crease in his trousers, along with the gold fob chain dangling from his vest, screamed wealth.

Derrick's fingers itched to snatch the pocket watch, so he gripped the wall harder. Even he wasn't that bold. If the gent were on a toot, he'd be the perfect fodder. But from the straight rod jammed up his arse, he hadn't had a drop.

Derrick narrowed his eyes on him. "How can I help you?" He couldn't fathom what he could do for the likes of such a bluenose. But it wouldn't do to offend him. The man was tall and wiry, probably capable of belting him if the wrong word slipped out.

"Does a Lady Margaret sing here?"

Every dolt knew Lady Margaret *sang* here. Derrick's insides lit up like a tree on Christmas. He could be an agent or someone important. "Guess you ain't from around here, huh? What do you want with Lady Margaret? You an agent? A producer?" Too bad Ira had him thrown out of the club, he might have let the egg buy him a couple of drinks. He looked flush enough to afford it.

"You know her?" His eyes lit up. He seemed too jazzed for it to be about business. Maybe he was Lady Margaret's sheik?

Derrick grunted. A man in pursuit of his lover was an unlikely source for hooch. "I've been known to take in her show now and then."

"Is she here?"

"You ain't gone in to see?" Yes was the easy answer, but why give him information if there was nothing in it for him?

The man's mouth twisted. "I don't have the password."

Derrick resisted rubbing his hands together. The man was entirely at his mercy. "If you're buying, I can get you in."

"She's here?"

"Her set's about over."

"Good, perhaps she has information about Lady Charlotte Leighton."

Derrick's body went rigid at the slightly familiar name. "Who?"

"Lady Charlotte Leighton, my *fiancée*." The man reached inside his coat and pulled out a photo. "This is she."

Derrick stared at a picture where sad, soft eyes stared back. Full lips turned down, hair pulled tightly away from her face. He definitely knew this woman. Except now her hair was cut short so that it curled round her shoulders. Charli. "I'm sorry, did you, uh, say fiancée?"

"Yes, she went missing six months ago." He drew a hand through perfectly groomed hair. "We'd no idea what happened. Her parents and me. Then I stumbled across this." He reached inside his coat a second time and tugged out a folded newsprint. He pointed to an article with the headline A *Rising New Star Is On The Horizon.* Derrick had seen the article days ago. He'd lusted after the photo of Lady Margaret. "Lady Margaret was a school chum of Charlotte's. I thought perhaps they, um, that they may have traveled together."

Derrick leaned into the cool brick and shut his eyes. Charli was a runaway. More importantly, she was an heiress, judging from the looks of her fiancé. Endless possibilities swirled through his head, making him dizzy. But how to spin the situation? Blackmail the parents? Nah, that wouldn't work. London was too far away to pull off such a scam.

Still, Charli had run from *this* man. Derrick would wager every buck he could get his hand on that this skinny, proper twig wasn't her type.

He eyed him again. Maybe he was cruel. Not all evil men lurked under a rough exterior. Some were well-dressed, handsome dicks with deceptively mild manners. A small, satisfied grin filled him. None of that mattered as long as there was profit in it.

Derrick fingered the hilt of his knife. Smooth and solid. More than enough to rid this man of his cabbage. "I know her. She's a waitress at Club 501, but this is, uh, her off night. Why don't you meet me back here tomorrow, and I'll get you in to see her."

"Thank you." The man grabbed Derrick's hand and shook it enthusiastically. "Thank you. You can't possibly know how much I appreciate your assistance. I won't rest until I know she's back home safe."

"It's my pleasure." Derrick grinned. In a little while this egg wouldn't be feeling so great. He slipped his hand back into his pocket, fingers curling around his knife. The cold, firm handle lent him courage for the task ahead. The night hadn't turned into such a waste after all. Things were looking up. Derrick waited until the man turned the corner. Then followed.

****

Charli sagged against the brick façade outside of Club 501 and rubbed the back of her neck. What a tedious night. She hadn't even the energy to change from her uniform. With a deep breath, she gathered her strength for the walk home, making a mental note of the items she still needed from the street vendors. Milk, butter, blueberries, and sugar. Her wages from the night should cover the cost with just enough left over for her portion of rent. Her footsteps lightened. If only she could speak with Mrs. Carter—

"Charlotte?" The familiar nasal voice stopped her as surely as a band of iron bracing her against a wall.

Geoffrey!

It couldn't possibly be. She'd traveled an ocean to rid herself of that nightmare. She whirled, her heart sinking when her eyes confirmed what her mind already knew. "W-w-what are you doing here?"

How? How had he found her? She swallowed.

With three long strides the man she thought to never lay eyes on again closed the distance between them. Her spirits sank with every step. A cell door slammed on her short-lived freedom. He wrapped his spindly fingers around her arms, squeezing tightly. Too tightly. "Thank God. We thought we'd lost you." His breathy dramatics sickened her.

We, who? She squirmed from his grasp and met his gray eyes. Concern? How could a man who barely knew her be so concerned of her welfare? She grimaced. Her parents, of course. They put him up to locating her. Why couldn't everyone just leave her alone? "How did you find me?"

Geoffrey dug into his suit pocket and pulled out a wrinkled bit of newspaper. He smoothed it flat and held it out. She snatched it with numb fingers and moved under the streetlamp. A sensual, come-hither, if grainy, photo of Meggie beamed under the headline.

Oh no. Word had spread far. Her hand flew to her neck, her vision blurred.

"I followed the breadcrumbs you might say." His grin was much too satisfied.

"Oh." The only word she could manage from her constricted throat.

He grabbed her shoulders and shook. "Why would you leave? Did your school chums force you?"

"No! Of course not." How utterly ridiculous. His grip tightened as a hard glint reflected in his eyes.

His gaze traveled over her uniform, her newly shorn hair. She clasped her hands together, resisting the urge to cover herself from his scrutiny. Needle pricks ricocheted up her spine. This was it. He was here to drag her home. She chewed her lip.

"This is your dream? A life no better than a servant?" He eyed her garb with the venom of a pampered man who'd never known an honest day's work. "This is not you." He pointed to her now stained and wrinkled uniform. "You're nobility, for God's sake. This is far beneath your lot in life, Lady Charlotte."

How would he know? The precious son of her parents' friends. She hadn't even known him when they were children. Their first meeting was at their *engagement dinner*. Arranged marriages had been outdated since the early 1800s, *even in England*. Oh, how attentive he'd played, but she'd heard the rumors. Knew the front he presented would end the moment he slipped the manacle about her finger. Her duties for "serving" would shift to unpaid, planning parties, while he ran his household—and her—with an iron fist. Treating her as nothing more than a receptacle to bear his children. *His* property. She shivered. Serving illegal liquor to hoary-eyed patrons was the much better choice.

"I-I have nothing to say to you." She whirled and marched away from expectations that had besieged her since the day she was born.

Heart thumping, breathing shallow, Charli escaped. From him. From her previous life.

Loud, firm steps thundered behind her. What had she expected? The man had followed her from London. Fury pressed through her veins. Well, that was *his* choice. She hadn't asked him to look for her. But she couldn't...*wouldn't* go back to that life. She walked faster. Almost running, but strong fingers curled about her arm, jerking her to a stop.

"Charlotte." He gasped for air. "What the devil are you doing?"

"Getting away from you." Her hand flew to her mouth. Had those words just come out of *her*? Only six months in New York, and she'd gained gumption. From wherever the fortitude rose, she embraced it. Clung to it. Needed it. She yanked her arm from his grip, and before he could stop her, continued down the sidewalk. "Leave me alone."

"Why are you being so obstinate?" His voice echoed in the quiet of the night. Still, he trailed her. The familiar entrance to her flat lay only two blocks ahead. She pushed to close the distance—between Geoffrey and her old life—to reach her haven.

Almost there. All she required was the strong, unyielding door between herself and her blasted pursuer. If he persisted, she'd call the constable. Just see if she didn't. She was a free woman. This was America. The days of indentured servitude were over. His footsteps gained. His breath brushed her nape. She wasn't going to make it. She stretched out her arm as if an invisible chord could yank her to safety.

But his arms wrapped around her once more, keeping her from her refuge.

"No!" Her insides turned to jelly, and she dug her heels into the ground. But the hard surface offered no traction. She twisted, and his hold tightened.

"Stop this," he breathed in her ear. "You are creating a scene. I am not accosting you. I'm taking you home to London, where you belong."

"There's no one around to see it." Her heart swelled, pounding against her rib cage. She choked down the bitter taste of bile. "I'm not going with you." This was not happening. She dug her elbow into his abdomen. He grunted but didn't release her. He dragged her into the alleyway, pressed her against the wall. His eyes glittered in the darkness. All traces of the dignified nobleman fled. The monster reared its ugly head, the one she'd only heard of through rumors.

He shook her so hard her brain rattled. "Stop this instant. You are behaving like a child."

She clenched her jaw. *A child*? Wasn't traveling an ocean to force an unwilling person where they chose not to go treating her like a child? Refusing to give her a choice in the matter? She stilled. He let out a breath at her sudden acquiescence, and his hold loosened. She jammed her heel into his foot.

His hold dropped, he grabbed his foot, knee against his chest. "You little bitch!"

Charli backed away. "If you come near me, I'll scream."

Her threat seemed to amuse him. He dropped his foot and stalked to her. "You've no choice, Charlotte." His words were cool, confident. "The contracts have been signed. You are bound to me."

A shadow appeared behind him. "Don't think so, Brit. The lady gave you the icy mitt. Leave her alone."

"Slick?" Her mind whirled. The man who favored five finger discounts—*he* was her savior. But where had he come from?

Geoffrey spun, hands out. Moonlight glinted off a blade in Slick's hand.

Charli gasped. "What are you doing?"

"Protecting you, doll."

"What is the meaning of this, sir?" Geoffrey straightened into full blown British blubbery, offense ringing in every word. "This is my fiancée. She needs no protection from me."

"That's not what I see, fella."

"Slick, please. I-I'm fine. He's leaving." Slick's appearance increased the surge of adrenaline coursing through her veins. Now he knew where she lived. She turned to Geoffrey. "Right, Geoffrey?"

"Uh, of course. We can discuss this later." His tone promised she would not escape a second time.

"No." Slick's voice steeled into the most frightening growl she'd ever heard. So calm. So resolved. "I think a lesson is in order. Hand over your dough."

"Are you mad?"

"You're either gonna hand it over, or I'm gonna take it." He bared his yellow, wolf-like teeth. "And you ain't gonna like that."

Geoffrey lunged, and his fist landed with a loud thud against Slick's face. Slick stumbled back, his mouth tightening into a sneer. With a loud yowl he dove and thrust his knife into Geoffrey's stomach. A grunt left Geoffrey, followed by the sickening sound of the knife being pulled out of flesh.

Charli's world shifted into a horrific nightmare as Geoffrey staggered back, hands clamped on his gut, eyes wide and wild. He wilted to the sidewalk. Dark liquid oozed between his fingers, soaking his trousers. The acrid stench of blood saturated the night air. The knife clattered to the ground. A hard, brittle, unnatural sound. It reverberated around her hollow heart.

Charli ran to him and fell on the cold pavement, cradling his head on her lap. *Dear God.* "Geoffrey!" She leveled her gaze on Slick. "What have you done?" she whispered.

He shrugged as if he was a hero. "You wanted to stay, didn't you, doll? Now you can." A maniacal grin spread across his grotesque features. His gaze moved to Geoffrey's sputtering form.

Geoffrey kicked the ground, arched his back. Gasping. Grunting. Gurgling for what seemed an eternity. The world and her former fiancé stilled.

Slowly, reality set in. Her arms tingled with the weight of Geoffrey's head, and tears spilled down her face. "I never asked for this." Her hand smoothed his hair back from his ashen face. Eyes closed, his mouth open in a wide, silent scream. Comprehension scorched her heart, burned her throat. Her vision dimmed. "Y-you killed him."

"I saved you from whatever it is you were running from." He bent down, lifted her away from Geoffrey's still form.

A chill hit her nerves where he touched her. Freezing her in place. She couldn't move. Couldn't breathe. Couldn't think.

"Now you're safe." His eyes burned with an unidentifiable light. He appeared more present than she'd ever seen him. More alive.

Somehow, the smallest bit of logic surfaced from the chaos raging inside. "We have to call the constable."

"You don't want to do that, doll." Slick jabbed a finger at her. "Who do you think they'll look at first? The man said he knew you."

"But I-I-I didn't do anything."

He arched a brow. So cool. Ending a life didn't bother him at all. He pointed to the uniform. Soaked splotches dotted the sheer material. Smaller spots trailed her apron up to her waist. "How will you explain that blood on your dress? Even if they accept your excuse, you were here. And you did nothing to stop me."

She went numb from head to toe. She spun in a circle, helplessness crawling over her skin, through her veins. She couldn't go to jail. *She'd done nothing wrong.* "Stop you! How? How could I have stopped *you?*" Agonizing fear washed over her. "What am I going to do now?" A sob tore from her raw throat.

He took off his cloak and draped it around her. Some part of her shocked senses acknowledged the gentlemanly gesture. "Go home and change, honey. I'll take your jacket and apron now. Bring your bloody dress to work tomorrow. I'll dispose of them."

"What about…" She couldn't say it. She dragged her eyes from Geoffrey.

"I'll take care of the body. Now go."

Charli fled, guilt chasing her all the way. But still, she ran from Geoffrey's mangled body. Two bodies in as many days. She'd never seen a dead person in her life, and now…She shuddered and swallowed back nausea.

Slipping between the shadows, she bunched her skirt between tight fists, doing her best to conceal the dark spots. If only she could rip off her clothes this instant. Scrape away the reminder of Geoffrey's unyielding body—her participation in his death. Make things different. Tears clouded her vision. She tripped over a crack, nearly colliding with a lamppost. Palm against it, she dragged in ragged breaths.

Dear God, she'd wanted a different future. But one of her own making, and now she was suddenly a fugitive? Charli wrapped her arms around the steel post, pushed her cheek against the cold solid metal.

A giggle wafted from across the street, startling her. She glanced over quickly, expelling a relieved sigh. Only a couple, strolling hand in hand, gazing into one another's eyes. They didn't give a jot about a woman wearing a bloody dress. *Home.* She had to get home. Before they noticed her. Before anyone did.

Chapter Three

What was she going to do now? Her whole world was crumbling like a stale cookie with no way of reassembling the pieces. Last night she cursed her life as a mere cocktail waitress. Today her job would be a blessing if she could rewrite history so that Geoffrey was alive and on his way back to London. She yanked the hot pad off the counter and opened the oven door. Smoke filled the small kitchen. She coughed, waving until the smoke cleared. The tops of the pastries were golden brown, but a black rim framed their bottoms. Burnt! How could she fail at something she did automatically? Her shoulders slumped. All bad things came in threes. With two down, her chances of overcoming Slick's impulsive act were nil. Her vision blurred, lips quivering. Things would never be right again.

She removed the scones, examining the blackened bottoms, and piled them on a plate. They could scrape the sullied portion off. It wouldn't do to waste food. Her flatmates might not appreciate overcooked scones, but they were barely making ends meet as it was. She stared at the empty tray. Start another batch or toss the useless thing into the sink? No point. She was incompetent. Her throat burned with held-back tears. She let them flow. With all the fears she'd contemplated while boarding the *Empress of India*, it'd never occurred to her things would turn out like this. On the run. Alone. Hopeless.

Meggie entered the kitchen and wrapped her arms around Charli, laying her chin on her shoulder. "Charli, it's just a batch of scones. The next group will turn out fine. I'm certain of it." She brushed a strand of hair from Charli's face. Her soft hazel eyes shone with sympathy.

She knew Meggie was trying to comfort her, but something about her attempt sent white hot rage to the base of her neck. She shook her friend off. How dare she try to make her feel better? What could she know of Charli's situation? The woman who obtained everything she wanted and never had to suffer over a choice she'd made. Then there was Charli. Every decision she made turned wrong. She traveled here to be nothing more than a servant and now worse. Her brief glimpse of independence had turned nasty cold. Meggie was the wrong person to bring her solace, and she didn't deserve it anyway.

"No! It won't. Nothing will ever turn out right for me. Ever," she shouted. "You. You don't know anything, Lady *Perfect*." She slammed the baking sheet into the sink, then turned and dashed to her room. The sinister chill of remorse engulfed her the minute she pulled the curtains closed. She crumpled onto her bed, muffled broken sobs escaping into the linens. The horrid way she'd treated her friend intensifying her pain. What an ungrateful, wretched person she'd become. One catastrophic event, undeniably a doozy, turned her into an insolent child. She lay on the sodden sheets until she'd no tears left.

A faint snore pulled her from her from her dark musings. Charli sat up. Good Lord, Eliza was sleeping in the bed across the room, her form barely discernable underneath the mound of blankets. A wisp of dark hair peeked from the edge of the sheet pulled over her head, her bare feet twisted in the linens base. Charli couldn't help but smile. Leave it to Eliza. Her slumber so deep and peaceful, Charli's sobs would never wake her. Charli took a long breath and squared her shoulders.

No matter what happened next, she would face it with dignity. The cage hadn't snapped shut yet. And if it did, she wouldn't punish her friends. She sat up and smoothed the wrinkles of her skirt. It was time to make things right with Meggie.

She crossed the tiny flat to the room Meggie and Jess shared and eased the curtain open. Meggie was sound asleep. Charli wouldn't disturb her rest but resolved to address her rudeness later. She took a deep breath and reentered the kitchen, then gathered the ingredients for a new batch of scones.

She grasped a pair of knives. She sliced cold butter, pressing the blades so close they bent. Churning butter and flour into a lumpy mass was the hardest part of making scones, and that suited her just fine. Anything to get her mind off Geoffrey lying limp and lifeless on the hard asphalt. She bit her lip, concentrating on the screech of the knives folding the ingredients into one. Her arms burned at the effort, but she pushed through it. The first batch had already burned. This one would be flawless.

She wiped her flour-dusted arm across her forehead. Breathed in the obnoxious smell of burnt scones, refusing to lose focus this time. No matter what, last night's events wouldn't undermine her baking. Not a second time. The kitchen was normally the only place she was truly at peace. Not today. Guilt and revulsion tainted every action. Robbed her of the joy she tried to muster from her task. Her vision blurred, and the image of a blood-crusted knife and the gurgle of Geoffrey's lungs rose unbidden. She'd never be the same again. She felt as empty as a sack without flour. Her whole life she dreamed of being a baker, having her own shop. Now, she would lose not only her dream but her freedom. Even more devastating, she'd watched Geoffrey die.

"Where is she?" Jessica's strident voice jerked Charli to the present. Her flatmate breezed into the room waving her paper in the air. Charli bit back the desire to scream. Whatever could be so urgent that had Jess bolting into the room shrieking at the top of her lungs? But she'd vented her rage at one friend too many today. She wasn't up to a repeat. That was one thing she had control over. Besides, Jessie had probably been out chasing after some tasty nugget for one of her stories. That accounted for her need to have her questions answered instantly. She was doing what she came to New York to do—ferret out real news. Her friend hadn't witnessed a murder or tried to cover up her sins.

"Afternoon, Jess. If you're looking for Meggie, she's sleeping." Charli tried to put a bright note into her voice. A fat lot of good it did. Her tone was flat and listless. She kept her focus on the task at hand, though she could feel Jess's gaze burning through her. Her expression on high alert. Jess's journalist instincts had kicked in.

"Drat! I need to talk to her." Jess removed her coat revealing a stylish sea green suit that enhanced the red highlights in her hair then turned back to Charli. "Is something the matter?"

Charli's throat closed. In spite of the urge to blurt out everything, she daren't utter a word. What if she were thrown in prison? In a foreign country? She couldn't tell Jess what Slick had done. Charli was the one with bloody clothes. Certainly, Slick would find a way to weasel out of his misdeeds just like he did everything, and she would be the one left facing charges. No one would believe her innocent. She clamped her jaw so tightly it ached.

Jess strolled over to the counter where the last batch of blueberry scones sat piled high on a plate. She snatched one up and wrinkled her nose. "Now I know something is up." She whirled on Charli. "You burned the scones. You never do that. Spill!"

There was no getting away from Jess's intense scrutiny. Once she caught on to the least bit of intrigue, she pursued it like a hound tracking a fallen grouse. Charli's mind spun. There had to be something that would distract Jess. Then her eyes lit on a bit of newsprint clutched in Jess's hand. "What's that you're holding?"

"That's what I need to talk to Meggie about." Jess's eyes grew wide, a hint of intrigue dancing within. "You'll never guess what I found…" Jess frowned. "Oh no you don't. You're trying to distract me. Out with it."

Charli sighed. Her hands twisted the apron sash. What quandary *could* she be embroiled in that would satisfy Jess's curiosity? Mrs. Carter! "You remember the department store lady, Mrs. Carter?"

"Vaguely."

"Well yesterday I learned she wanted to add a bakery in the center of her store." Charli waited. Assessed her friend's response. Jess looked appeased, so Charli rushed on. "I-I wanted to give her a sample of my scones. Hoping she would take me on—you know…as the baker. Now they're ruined. My scones are ruined." To her horror, her lips quivered and tears slid down her cheeks. Again!

"Oh, Charli. Mrs. Carter will love your scones. Look." She examined the pastry. "They're only burnt on the bottom. We can scrape that part off. Make another batch. I'm sure they'll be perfection."

"Thanks." Charli expelled a breath. Her insides curdled at how easily the lie slipped off her tongue. What a horrid thing to have to do. If she didn't make good on her little fib, she'd be no better than a con artist. The more she thought about it, the better the idea became. She actually smiled and marched back to the stove with a renewed purpose.

A sound at the doorway made Charli look up. Eliza entered the kitchen and filled the tea kettle. "What the devil is going on?" Her light brown eyes held a wariness that seemed permanent lately.

She'd been acting so strangely. In spite of her new position, nice clothes, fancy shoes, she seemed dejected. Those things should have brought her joy. But each passing day, her mouth turned farther downward. Her shoulders drooped lower. It was as if she were readying herself to attend a funeral.

"Meggie!" Jess showed Eliza the paper. "She's truly lost her senses."

27

Eliza studied the paper, then looked at Jess. "Meggie was involved in some kind of...shootout?"

"It appears so." Jess took the paper and headed to the room she shared with Meggie.

Shootouts? Stabbings? What on Earth? At least Meggie was okay, regardless of what had transpired last night. She was resting peacefully when Charli checked on her. Perhaps Jess was exaggerating.

Charli returned to her batter. She willed her muscles to relax, falling into the familiar rhythm of mixing. Despite the wretched events of the previous night, excitement bubbled inside her. Why hadn't she thought to offer Mrs. Carter a sample long ago? No matter. She'd do it now. Her baking career was about to catapult her to success. Who said you had to have a great voice to be an overnight sensation?

****

Detective Noble slipped past the two field officers blocking the entrance into a narrow alleyway. Though it was four in the afternoon, the sun's golden rays did nothing to illuminate the corridor. A strong gust of wind as cold as the dead body dumped at the end of the alley pressed against Felix's back, urging him toward an investigation with flimsy evidence. No wonder they sent him. Another crime. Most likely another dead end.

He picked his way through crumpled newsprint, discarded boxes, and a foul, unidentifiable ooze. The sour smell of yesterday's garbage accompanied each breath. He jerked a handkerchief from his pocket, covered his nose, and managed to inhale as little as possible. He strolled to the far end where Redburn jotted notes on a small pad next to the lifeless form.

The victim, dressed in an expensive suit, lay on his back, neck twisted at a sharp angle. His arms were sprawled across the pavement and legs bent over an empty box. A wealthy man on *this* side of town? The man was too far north to be a rum runner. Perhaps he'd made a different kind of shady deal. Whatever the explanation, the egg came out on the wrong end. A man of his sort wouldn't have shown up here unless he were up to no good.

"What do we have?"

Redburn crouched next to the body and glanced up at Felix. "Not much, Detective. This one's clean. No identification, no money or jewelry. Looks like a mugging turned nasty."

Felix stooped next to the officer. A large blood-soaked spot stained the victim's suit coat. Felix peeled back the linen jacket. A narrow slit in the base of the white shirt was drenched with blood. "Stab wound. Any idea how long he's been here?"

"Nah, he was discovered by a trash collector this afternoon. We've canvassed the neighborhood. There are scattered reports of an argument between a man and woman early this morning, but no one was sure of the time."

"Anybody see anything?"

"Nope."

"Jesus, you'd think someone would show curiosity at all the ruckus."

Redburn shook his head. "They thought it was a lover's spat. Nothing to get into a twist over."

Felix's eyes adjusted to the dimness. He peered down the length of the alley. Trash littered the area with the exception of an uneven path through the center. "Was any trash collected from the dumpster today?"

"Nope. The trash collector was instructed not to disturb the area. Nothing has been removed since the body was found."

Felix rolled the victim to his side. The back of his jacket and bottom of his trousers appeared worn, the heels of his shoes scuffed. "Looks like he was dragged here."

Felix dropped him, rose, and followed the trail to the exit. Dried blood coated the mouth of the alley. He scratched his chin. "The mugger must have cornered and stabbed the man just inside the alley then dragged him out of sight." He scanned the street, knowing how futile the act was. There were no answers on the pavement. No abandoned car in the vicinity. Had the man taken a cab or walked? He was certainly naïve to travel alone in a foreign neighborhood. A foolish act that left him open to an easy assault.

"Hey, Detective," one of the officers manning the crowd said as Mike Mulligan swaggered through the mass of people. "Heard you nailed the Hyde Park Strangler."

"Guilty as charged." He pointed a triumphant finger at the officer.

"So what's that? Three murders this month?" The officer beamed at Mulligan. If this had been anything other than a murder scene, he'd be paying homage to a king. Felix grimaced. The last thing he needed was a detective who preferred shortcuts to real investigative work.

"Fifth." Mike glanced at Felix. "I'm on a roll."

Just like the bastard to rub it in. Felix nodded with enough curtness to ice the alley. No need to encourage the guy. Mulligan was arrogant enough without confirmation that his dig hit Felix hard. Unlike Mulligan, Felix refused to cross ethical lines. If that meant a wrongdoing remained unsolved to keep innocents out of prison, so be it. He solved cases by following the trail of evidence. Not manufacturing proof.

"Hey." Mike sauntered over to Felix. "The captain sent me over to assist you."

"How did I get so lucky?" Felix bit out the words, perusing the scene for anything he might have missed.

"No need to get all balled up. Just following orders."

Felix glanced back at Mike. His conciliatory tone didn't diminish the wicked gleam in his eyes.

"Cap'n thinks you've allowed too many cases to pile up. So…" He lifted a shoulder. "I'm here to help."

"Don't know how much help you could be. I prefer reliable methods to crime solving." Felix flexed his hand, tempted to plant a fist into Mike's smug mug. But engaging in a pissing match with the department's golden boy was not the most desirable way to get attention.

"Whatever gets the job done, right?" Mike winked.

Felix turned his back on the preening peacock and headed to the body.

Mike followed, matching his stride. "Most of my cases end in confessions. That's how to get results."

Felix stopped, met Mike's steel gray eyes. "A confession under duress is not only unreliable, but highly unethical."

"Oh yeah?" Mike grinned. "Innocent people don't confess. Everyone knows that."

Felix grunted and resumed his walk.

Mike scowled. "You can be as pious as you want. But how many cases have you closed this month? Your *reliable* methods are a load of shit."

Felix shook his head. "I'm lead detective on this case. We'll do things my way."

"We'll see."

Felix didn't bother responding. He had nothing more to say. Mike curled his lips, baring yellowed teeth. The guy was ready for a fight, and Felix bit back a grin. Hell, he couldn't figure what Mike was so sore about. The man was on top. The darling of the police department. If Felix was a threat to him, then he considered it a compliment.

Redburn greeted Mike with a curt nod. Guess he wasn't the only one who thought Mike's ego was bigger than the city. Felix relaxed.

Mike looked at the dead man. "This guy's out of place for this neighborhood."

Redburn stood, back straight, legs spread, hands braced beneath his armpits. "He could have a bit of fluff in these parts."

"Suppose that's possible." Felix nodded. "If that were the case, he should have had transportation. Find out if there has been an abandoned or stolen car reported in this vicinity."

If there was, they could likely identify the man. His attire spelled undue wealth. Someone must miss him. When he got back to the precinct, he'd peruse the missing person reports. On the off chance they'd overlooked something, Felix crouched one last time to examine the lining of the man's jacket. He ran his fingers along the inside fold. A small thrill of anticipation skittered up his spine. *Stiff, like a folded piece of paper*. Felix pulled the knife from his trouser pocket and flipped out the blade and cut along the seam. With a gentle tug, he pulled out the slip of paper. GEOFFREY HARE, 9242 Wimple Street, London, England.

A surge of victory coursed through him. Now he was getting somewhere. Knowing the man's identity, Felix could retrace his steps. This was just the case to set his career back on track.

Chapter Four

Felix wasn't surprised to be walking through a speakeasy door. Murder, mayhem, and criminal activity thrived in the gin joints these days. No matter how prettily they packaged it, selling hooch was still against the law. But he couldn't forge a real connection between the victim's noble London lineage and this seedy warehouse. "Are you sure we're at the right place?"

"Of course we are." Mike looked down his nose at him. "No self-respecting businessman puts a speakeasy in an obvious place. Keeps the coppers away, you know."

Felix grimaced. Mike was much too comfortable with the illicit side of life. The man he'd drawn as partner stood with his shoulders squared and chest puffed out. Felix clenched his jaw, seized with an urge to deflate the man's ego along with his nose. How had someone like Mike risen so quickly up the police force ranks? He was commissioned with the duty to suppress illegal activity, not embrace it. It negated all reason. "You have the password?"

"Don't worry, everything's Jake." Mike rapped on the door. Three firm confident knocks.

Wood grated against wood, revealing a sliver of an opening.

"Elephant's eyebrows."

Felix's lips twitched. Nonsense, pure nonsense. He shook his head. Criminals got more creative every day. After a long pause, the door swung open.

"Come on," Mike said.

Felix followed Mike down a dark staircase into a dimly lit room, jaw dropping. The place was huge. A long mahogany bar filled one side of the room, leaving the other side open for table seating and hordes of people in the center dancing. His eyes drifted up to a mezzanine. High-pitched voices mingled with rich baritones. Screeching laughter and loud guffaws punctuated the smooth jazz sounds of a small six-piece band. He knew these places were popular, but they violated everything Felix believed in. And to find the place filled to the baseboards, leaving no clear path to edge through, sent a surge of fury through him. He and Mike forged their way to the bar.

"Ira." Mike motioned to the bartender. "We need a word with ya."

"What? Can't you see I'm busy?" the man shouted over the hubbub.

Felix pulled the photo he'd confiscated from Hare's abandoned hotel room. The swanky Ritz on upper 5th Avenue, no less. With clenched teeth, he waited somewhat impatiently for the bartender to wind his way over. Felix had half a mind to yell "raid." Ah, but that was not the mission here.

Ira wiped his hands on a towel at his waist and sauntered over. "Make this quick, will ya? You can see how busy we are."

Felix flipped out his badge. "Ira, is it? I suggest you drop the attitude, *Ira.* We have some questions."

A measure of satisfaction crept over Felix at the bartender's tightened lips. He glanced around before giving a short nod.

"We need to know if either of these individuals look familiar to you." He held out the sepia image of Hare photographed with a woman, his supposed fiancée.

According to the victim's parents, the marriage was arranged. Shortly thereafter, she disappeared. From their incipient description of the event, they viewed her absence an act of defiance. Not foul play.

Duty must be a dark and insidious word. An arranged marriage in this day and age seemed ancient, barbaric. The woman in the photo looked oddly familiar. Her dark, sorrow-filled eyes struck something deep inside. As if she were facing the gravity of a life sentence rather than a future of wedded bliss. She was a choice bit of calico with soft features and a slim frame. There was nothing to indicate any real grit in the woman. Yet somehow she found the courage to run. Felix chastised himself. Photos never revealed someone's true nature.

Ira's gaze shifted from the photo to Felix. He rubbed his chin. "Why do you want to know?"

"I'm investigating the man's murder."

Ira's eyes widened. He held out his hands in a placating gesture. "Hold on. I ain't got nothing to do with this."

Mike leaned in. "Ira. We don't care about the booze. Right, Felix?"

Felix surveyed the club with disgust but relented. "Right." On the hierarchy of crimes, murder ranked higher than the illegal sale of alcohol. But overlooking one transgression to gain insight on another didn't sit too well in Felix's book. Just because Mike had informed him that this establishment was working with the police on a sting operation didn't make the place any less repugnant.

Ira furrowed his brow, suspicion cloaking his features.

"You're not a person of interest or under arrest," Felix said. *At least not yet.* "I just need to know if you can identify these people."

Ira glanced back at the photo. He pointed to Hare. "I've never seen this guy before." His finger moved over the woman. "But the dame looks like Charli. She's cut her hair, but that's her."

"Any idea where we might find her?"

Ira laughed. A menacing sound that sent a shot of apprehension up Felix's spine. "Just look over your shoulders, fellows." He laughed again and sauntered back to the bar.

*****

Charli grabbed her tray and lost herself in the chatter of patrons and the blare of Bernie's horns. The night started rather more serenely than Charli expected. She'd handed over her blood-soaked clothes to Slick, who assured her he'd taken care of everything. A new apron hung in her cubby. A small gasp escaped. She hadn't even thought about how she would explain a missing apron. Now she didn't have to. Thank God. She grimaced. Slick's uncanny ability to be everywhere was a bit unnerving. She'd never taken him very seriously, but she would certainly not make that mistake again.

Serving her drinks with a speed she didn't know she possessed, the customers blurred into formless shapes. Nothing clear. No one identifiable. But all semblance of their anonymity faded with a light tap on her shoulder. She whirled around, and all breath left her. A man with blond hair, blue eyes, and spectacles placed an empty glass on her tray. Geoffrey? No. Geoffrey was dead.

"Might I have another?"

The similarity to Geoffrey took her breath away. She trembled as the horrific events of the previous night slammed her. With a jolt, the images she'd forced into the nether regions of her mind came flooding back. Not Geoffrey. She forced a steady breath, but Geoffrey's lifeless body wouldn't fade from her mind. His life's blood draining from his body. His pale empty eyes. She stumbled back, but the man caught her before she fell. "Are you all right, miss?"

She swallowed. "Yes. Another drink? Right away, sir." On shaking legs she rushed to fill the order, tears threatening. Logically, she *knew* she wasn't the one to end Geoffrey's life, yet—she could have, *should* have stopped Slick.

How could she have been so stupid not to see it coming? She sucked in a breath, squeezed her hands into fists to quell their trembling, and straightened. She had to find a way to carry on. She had to. All this acting like nothing was wrong? *Intolerable*. It was enough to drive one to Bedlam. She prayed for the day when the sight of the constable didn't send chills through her veins.

"Hey, Charli." Ira's irritated voice jolted her to the present. Ira pointed at the tray full of freshly made drinks, then to the tables. "I don't pay you to loiter. Get these drinks moving."

"Yes, sir." She balanced the tray on her shoulder. Doing things as she always did. Smiling at rude customers. Nodding when they ordered more. Pretending. Everything was fine.

Drinks delivered, she headed to the bar. And stopped. Two men stood with Ira. Heads bowed together in earnest conversation.

Her heart thudded. No. They surely weren't questioning Ira about her. Street clothes donned their bodies, not uniforms. Regular gents. But still, there was an unusual feel in how Ira deferred to them. A cringing, groveling wish to please, and it alarmed her. Her imagination swept her into fear. Slick assured her there was nothing that would lead back to the speakeasy. She watched transfixed as Ira scrutinized something the taller of the two held. From his unrelenting expression, he did not relinquish possession. The man nodded.

Ira laughed, then pointed in her direction.

Her mouth went dry. The tall one extricated himself from the conversation and turned his focus on her.

Panic choked her. She glanced about wildly. Her eyes flew to the secret paneled door. Could she make it? But his steady gait in her direction made running no longer an option.

"Miss Leighton?" His rich baritone sent danger signals through her body. *Focus.* She had to stay focused. She bit the inside of her cheek to clear her head. "I'm Detective Noble. May I have a few minutes of your time?"

Dots swamped her vision. The unruly crowd seemed to steal the oxygen. Frozen into place, she took deep, steady breaths. But it was no use, the world darkened, and she swayed. A strong hand gripped her elbows.

"Steady there." The detective guided her to the back room to a chair. She sank down, grateful for the solid wood beneath her bum. "Stay here."

He disappeared and returned with a glass of water. She took it, favoring him with a weak smile. The cool liquid slid down her throat. Wits. She needed to keep her wits about her. Detective Noble pulled up a chair next to her and reached into his inside pocket, pulling out a note pad. He handed her a newspaper clipping. Her engagement announcement.

"W-where did you get this?" Her voice was but a whisper.

The clipping was wrinkled and worn at the sides. She swallowed. The air whooshed from her body. Dizziness blurred her vision, and no air passed through her throat.

Dear God. *Don't faint. Don't faint. Don't faint.*

In the middle of Club 501. She would be sacked for certain.

"Is this you?" He pointed at her likeness taken so long ago. On a different path. Things had changed so much since then. She was independent. *Witness to a murder.* Her hand shook. She was never one to fabricate well. Like the time she'd spotted Jess and Meggie stuffing glue into the locks on finals day at Mrs. Greensley's School for Young Ladies. Monsieur Duclaric had badgered Charli until she'd confessed, crying all the while. A secret she still kept close to her heart.

Charli took another deep breath. "Yes, that's me."

"You're engaged to this man?"

She looked away. "Not any longer."

"The engagement was broken before you came here?" His voice held a frown, and she glanced back at him.

"Not exactly."

"Perhaps you'd care to explain then?"

He scribbled a few notes before meeting her gaze. His eyes narrowed as if he suspected something. Guilt choked her. She blew out a long breath. "My parents arranged the marriage between us. They felt I would never marry without their interference. But he and I were barely acquainted. I-I just couldn't do it—marry him. So I left. I…ran away."

"Are you telling me you came all the way to New York just to avoid marriage?" His lips twitched.

She pursed her lips and let out a stream of air. "You haven't met my parents."

****

Any notion Felix held that this woman had moxie fled. Running away was an act of avoidance not defiance. Her hands shook, her lips trembled. Lovely green eyes darted around the room. A sudden urge to take her hands in his and still their quaking barraged him. He shoved *that* inappropriate thought away. And then it hit him. She was one of the crowd surrounding Roxy Gould's body. He'd had that same inexplicable desire to offer comfort.

He studied her tightly fisted hands. Charlotte Leighton was hiding something. Was it only her runaway status, or was it murder?

He cleared his throat. "Your parents must be ogres."

"You've no idea." She chewed her lower lip. The tiny, insignificant action had warmth blossoming in his gut. He wrestled against the tightness banding his chest. What was it about this woman that stirred his body into reacting to her every move? "Did Geoffrey send you to find me?" The shy words pricked him. It could all be a ruse. Murder was a serious crime.

"No." Felix paused, considered his next words. "Were you aware he was in town?"

"In town?" Her eyes widened, and her hand flew to her throat. Whatever she was mixed up in, her fear was real. "Please, don't tell him you found me." She whispered the plea.

Felix couldn't fathom the woman across from him as a killer. She was too fragile. Stabbing Hare on her own? He didn't believe it. She was too skittish to contemplate murdering anyone. Even in self-defense. An unbidden desire to protect her surged. But he squelched it. Charlotte Leighton might be beautiful with innocent doe eyes, but not only was she a person of interest, she was his main suspect. And he had a career to salvage.

Despite his gut instincts, professional distance took precedence. "I regret to inform you that Mr. Hare was found dead early this morning." He said the words gently and gaged her reaction.

"Dead? I-I don't understand." Miss Leighton's lower lip quivered. One lone tear slipped down her cheek. "What happened?"

"We believe he fell victim to a mugging."

"What?" The word came out a whisper. She sniffed. He dug out his handkerchief and stuffed it in her hand. She dabbed her eyes. "Poor Geoffrey."

"Look, Miss Leighton." He handed her his card. "If you think of anything to help, please call me." Old instincts clashed with cold reality. Charlotte Leighton didn't appear evasive, but Felix knew there was more to her than met the eye.

Chapter Five

Charli reentered the main room, wiping away the tears from her cheeks. She skirted the wall searching for her tray. Slick cornered her, standing too close, one hand on the wall, trapping her. His breath reeked of sour alcohol. Her stomach roiled.

"What'd the copper want?"

Charli gripped her hands together. How easily Slick barged his way into her life. Until this mess was finished, there'd be no shaking him. Her gaze darted about for escape. Her best avenue for a reprieve was Ira, but he wasn't behind the bar. She licked her lips. "He asked me about Geoffrey."

His eyes narrowed to slits. Funny. She'd never seen him as menacing before last night. Now, no matter what he did, she quivered. "And what'd you say?"

"Nothing. I told him I didn't know anything." Panic surged at his proximity.

"How'd they find out who the stiff was so fast?"

"I-I don't know." She focused on her hands. That was more comfortable than looking into the eyes of a cold-blooded killer.

"They suspect anything?"

Words flew from her mouth in a torrent. "He had an announcement of my engagement. Somehow they found me. What am I going to do?"

"Huh. Dig out those charms you have hiding. There's plenty a dame like you can use to your advantage."

Burning heat flooded her cheeks. Thank goodness the speakeasy was dimly lit so no one would see her shame.

"Whatever you do." Slick leaned in closer. "Keep your mouth shut." He glared at her, then stumbled away.

Charli's stomach lurched. She'd gotten herself into a pickle with no clear way out. Her legs wobbled. She forced deep breaths. In, out. In, out. Once steadier on her feet, she picked up her tray and darted to the bar. Ira was back, wiping it down. He didn't scold her. He didn't say anything at all. His silence unnerved her. Her life had turned upside down. Things would never be normal again.

****

Once back at the station, Felix sat at his desk, poring over his notes and documents. So far he had one big goose egg as far as any useful leads. Just some rich Brit who'd come to New York to retrieve his runaway fiancée. And wound up dead.

Miss Leighton wasn't too keen on marriage, but did that provide enough motive to kill him? He tapped his chin with an index finger. Maybe, maybe not. But it was enough to bring her in for further questioning.

He might even wrangle a confession out of her, but just like he'd told Mike, he preferred more reliable methods. Her trembling, crying over her dead fiancé, struck him as genuine. And though he knew he should, he couldn't squelch that urge to protect her. She needed help not persecution.

Still, gut instinct was never wrong. She held back something. He was positive of that. If only he could get her to trust him enough to tell him something.

Mike clapped him on the back and slid onto the corner of his desk. "Any progress with the canceled stamp?"

"Watch it," Felix barked. The amusement on Mike's face had him clearing his throat. He tugged his collar from his neck. "Uh, other than her connection to the victim, I've got nothing."

"Oh, come on." Incredulity swam in Mike's hard eyes. "The man traveled across the pond to find her and winds up dead. She works in the neighborhood. That's not a coincidence."

"I don't think she is capable of murder."

"Oh, please. Lots of women can kill given the right motivation." Mike shuffled through the file like they were truly in accord. But he wasn't privy to Felix's thoughts. Mike hadn't seen the woman's chin quiver at the news of her fiancé's demise. Though she hadn't appeared in love with the man, she was genuinely upset. She'd sincere tears. He'd seen enough fake ones to spot a woman's real cry. Even if he didn't doubt her guilt, there wasn't enough evidence to accuse her outright.

"Generally, women use poison or guns, not knives. Too physical. Anyhow, Miss Leighton doesn't have the strength to drag a man's body to the end of an alleyway."

"I don't know. People find the strength to do incredulous things under stress."

Coming from a man who wasn't against planting evidence to convict a wrong suspect, Mike's words burned with validity. Miss Leighton was their *only* lead. If they didn't come up with another connection, he'd be forced to bring her in. "I'm not convinced."

"Let's bring her in." Mike winked. "I'll get her to confess."

"We've had this conversation."

Mike snatched the picture of Officer Riley off his desk. Felix grabbed for it, but Mike held it out of reach. "At some point you have to free yourself from the influence of the sainted officer. He worked the force years ago. Things are different now."

"Not that different." Felix pointed to the photo's resting place. "Put it back."

Mike rolled his eyes but set the photo of the man who should have been Felix's father back in place. "So what's next in your rules of investigation procedure?"

Felix rubbed his chin. "We search for an alternate hypothesis."

Mike's lips curved in his sly fox smile. "Maybe she had an accomplice."

Felix glared, but there was no convincing Mike once he'd latched onto a suspect. "Who would've helped her?"

"Ira mentioned that one of their regulars has gotten pretty chummy with her."

"And you're telling me this now?"

"I know how you don't like accusing the innocent." Mike shrugged.

"Very funny. Give me a name?"

"Derrick Chaunce. Goes by Slick." Mike's eyes glowed with the passion of a man lording his genius over a dunce.

It didn't help that Felix felt like an idiot. He ran a hand through his hair. Being partnered with this goober was bad enough. It rankled that Mike was looking like the better detective.

"According to Ira, Slick is considered a bit of a flour flusher. When he's not mooching off the clientele, he pilfers drinks from the staff. No one pays him much mind. Except for your Miss Leighton."

Felix considered Mike's information. "Might be she just has a good heart." Beneath her quaking, Miss Leighton's eyes shimmered with kindness. Not the uncharitable type. On the other hand, the scene unfolding in Felix's mind left a sick foreboding that curdled deep in his gut. One that showed Miss Leighton being played by street scum and unable to fight her way out.

Mike pulled at cuffs stiffened with a whole box of starch. The man spent too much time on his appearance. It got him noticed, apparently. Hm. Maybe Felix should consider obtaining a new, clean, pressed suit to impress the brass. He snorted. As if.

"The funny thing is," Mike went on, "they weren't so chummy a couple days ago. Up until then, Miss Leighton held the same opinion as everyone else. Now they're thick as thieves. Bets are it has something to do with our poor departed victim."

Felix's mind reeled at this unexpected piece of information. What a surprise his new partner was turning out to be. Perhaps a real detective lurked beneath the man's glib demeanor. Felix's respect climbed a notch, maybe two. He leaned forward, elbows on his desk. "I say it's time to pay this Mr.

Chaunce a visit. Tonight. The next few days I'm otherwise engaged."

Mike leaned in. "Got a date?"

"I wish," he muttered under his breath. "I'm attending President Coolidge's election party, and I have to find the right suit before the big day."

Mike shook his head. "Why are you wasting your time with that drivel?"

Felix grimaced, respect dropping back to his original assessment. "Voting is one of this country's finest privileges. The only time we can voice our opinion on the direction of our nation. I'd hardly call it drivel."

"Suit yourself." Mike slid off the desk and sauntered away.

Felix stared at his retreating back. Sometimes it was a waste explaining things to those who refused to listen.

****

Derrick cracked the door far enough to see who the hell was pounding at it and peered through the narrow gap. The same two weasels he'd seen flashing their badges in unison at Club 501. Damned bitch. She'd betrayed him. His heart beat wildly. He clutched his chest, prepared to fake a heart attack. Anything to avoid speaking to them.

"Mr. Chaunce," Felix said. "We'd like a word with you."

Derrick's eyes darted around his apartment for any avenue of escape. The only window faced the front with a five-story drop. The coppers would nab him before he could unlatch the damn thing. *Fuck.* "Uh, what can I do for you fine gentlemen?"

"This is Detective Noble, and I'm Detective Mulligan. We have a few questions."

Derrick narrowed his eyes, sizing the two men up. "What's this about?"

The blond, Noble, stood rigid, feet together, ice blue eyes searing him. His nose wrinkled as if he'd caught a foul stench. The bastard thought himself better than him? The other man wore a fine pinstripe suit. His stance was more relaxed, like he was shuffling cards at a poker game. His brown eyes reflected amusement. Not condescending. Nor insulting. Just plain enjoyment of his task, the cat playing with his prey.

"We understand you're acquainted with a Miss Charlotte Leighton."

"Who?" Heat flooded his face. A trickle of perspiration slid down his neck. He had to get his wits under control. It all rested on how much that little bitch told them. If she'd blurted out the whole story, they would arrest him on the spot. He inhaled deeply, allowing calm to settle, taking a moment to gather his thoughts. No cuffs appeared. Their stance was relaxed. She must not have said a word. They couldn't know much.

Noble pulled a photo from his inside pocket. "Recognize her?"

Derrick studied the photo, rubbing his chin. He didn't answer right away. The more time he took to formulate an answer, the more likely they'd believe how well he knew her. "She looks familiar, but I can't place her."

Detective Noble glared at him. "Come now, you've been seen cavorting with this woman." His direct no nonsense approach caught Derrick off guard. Maybe the man knew more than they let on. Feigning ignorance might not get him far with Noble. Mulligan didn't utter a word. Derrick pursed his lips. It was a battle of wits. Noble and Derrick then.

"I cavort with a lot of women. Not all of them that memorable."

Noble stepped closer, towered above him. He shoved the photo in his face. "Take a closer look." His steel resolve sent fear quivering up Derrick's spine.

Derrick remained steady, refused to step aside. No way would he offer an invitation. Fear cloaked him. They might find the bloodied apron hidden in the oak chest. One of the only remaining furnishings of his late father's estate. Only a few feet away. How clever he'd thought he was keeping the apron as leverage against Charli. He clenched his hands into fists to stem their shaking.

That was all he needed, Mulligan poking around while Noble kept Derrick hammered with questions. He wasn't a fool. That's how cops operated.

Some goddamned insurance policy that was turning out to be. Not such an ingenious plan if they discovered the apron.

If the heat got to an unhealthy level, it would be easy to point the blame at her. But the heat was at his apartment.

"Sorry, can't place her."

"Cut the crap." Detective Noble set his jaw, his eyes narrowed.

Derrick's insides twitched. Mulligan, who'd appeared the most amiable of the two, planted his legs wide. He fisted one hand into the other. Chin high. Eyes hardened with determination. Derrick pulled at his shirt collar and swallowed. He couldn't back down now. "I'm sorry, I don't…"

"She works at Club 501," Mulligan said.

"A place we understand you frequent," Noble said.

Derrick viewed the image of Charli. Even in black and white, he could tell she had red hair and green eyes. Her innocent face was filled with apprehension. He'd freed her of that fate, and the thanks he got was dicks knocking down his door, insinuating *things.* He licked his lips. Charli hadn't pointed the finger at him, but if it had come this far, it wouldn't be long. He'd take care of things—*her*—before it came to that. "Oh, now I remember. That's Charli. She's served me a few drinks before. That's all."

Noble narrowed his eyes. "We understand the last few days you've spoken with her more than once."

Derrick shook his head. "You saw her, didn't you? All I want is the same as any other fella. Something sweet to sink—"

Detective Noble's fist slammed into his chin. Pain ricocheted through Derrick's jaw. He staggered back. The acrid taste of blood trickled over his tongue.

"What the hell do you think you're doing?" Detective Mulligan pulled Noble behind him. He turned to Derrick. "You'll have to forgive my partner. This case has him in a lather. If you think of anything else, let me know."

"Whatever you say, Officer." Derrick rubbed his swollen lip. He should threaten to sue. But a facer was the least of his problems. This was all Charli's fault. He'd make her pay. Once he planted the apron, her sorry ass would be locked up. Very sad, but better her than him.

Chapter Six

Carrying a full tray of drinks, Charli placed a glass of gin before a bleary-eyed, lone man at a corner table. The club was packed tonight with Meggie's throaty rendition of S*moke Gets in Your Eyes* rending the air. Even during slow songs, the floor was crowded with men and women—bodies pressed together, swaying to the music.

Charli made her way back to the bar, ready to trade empties for more full drinks. A loud crack sounded from the front door. Uniformed men spilled in amidst splintered wood. She let out a squeal.

"This is a raid!" The voice reverberated off the walls. "Everyone put your hands up."

Panicked, Charli glanced around. The room exploded into action. Meggie had disappeared from the stage and was nowhere to be seen. Jess no longer sat at the bar. People rushed around, shoving Charli like a bowling pin. Glasses tumbled over the edge of her tray, drenching her in fruit juice and gin. Her tray knocked away landed atop the shards, where they were stomped on by the club's patrons, scrambling in all directions.

Identifying anyone grew impossible. Charli spun, twisting in the chaos. Blurs of rose-, gold-, and green-clad bodies rushed past her.

"Get out of the way." An arm shoved Charli sideways, followed by another, pushing her into the mass of bodies flooding to the front. Charli gulped, propelled forward by the mob's momentum. Crushed in the center of an unstable mass of terror and alarm, she struggled to find room. Her chest collapsed, stifling the oxygen. She clawed at any potential opening, unable to extricate herself.

A small gap momentarily swelled open. Charli squeezed between two large men, shoving her way forward, and fled toward the back hallway. Another woman screamed in her ear, the sound reverberating against her eardrum in pain-tipped fear. Charli clamped her hands over her ears, brushing past the screecher. The crowd closed in, pressing her back into the stream of people desperate to escape.

Charli grabbed a wall corner, setting her feet firmly on the floor. But as hard as she tried to hold her ground, her fingers slipped from the hard surface. Her feet slid in the direction of the mob, impelling her up the staircase. Thrust out into the cool night air, she wrenched herself free. *Oh no.* Constables were everywhere, loading paddy wagons to overfilling.

Where was Meggie? Jess? She groped the side of the building, leaned against its smooth surface, gulping deep breaths. She squinted to focus. But everything was a blur. The only clear sight was the bright spots clouding her vision. Everything swayed. Anxious voices sounded muted, as if she were under water. The air was so thick she couldn't inhale. The fight within her dissolved. What was the point? She deserved jail, didn't she? Geoffrey was dead, and she'd allowed it. It was too much, just too much. Everything went dark. She slid down the wall.

"Careful there," a deep voice breathed against her cheek. Strong arms circled her, lifting her to her feet. "I've got you."

Charli relaxed into her rescuer, taking in a clean scent of cinnamon and cloves. The mingled spices reassured her, and her vision slowly cleared. She looked up into the cool eyes of Felix Noble.

"What are you doing here?" She shook her head, pushing away, freeing herself from his hold. That was a silly question. He was a constable. Why wouldn't he be here?

He crossed his arms, his lips curved in an amused smile. "Trying to help…" He peered intently, his voice low. "…you."

Applesauce! She poked a finger at him. "I don't want your help."

Whirling, she stumbled back to the chaos.

He gripped her hand and tugged her back. "You don't want to go that direction."

"Why not?"

"Because you'll be loaded up in one of those." He cocked his head to the jailed truck. "And carted to the station."

What was his motive? She narrowed her eyes on him. She didn't trust him. Not in the least. Perhaps being arrested was better than being alone with him. "Aren't you behind this?"

He shook his head. "Different unit. I came here looking for you."

It made absolutely no sense he would seek her out. Unless…her insides curdled like spoiled milk. This was about Geoffrey. She balled her hands into fists. "Looking for me? Why?"

"I thought I'd save you the trouble of spending the night in jail."

"W-w-what?"

"Thought you might need a ride home." He took her arm and led her toward a waiting vehicle. Her head spun trying to grasp this latest development. He wasn't going to arrest her. Surely more than her tray had been upended. There was no other explanation for his kindness.

****

Felix followed Miss Leighton into her apartment. There wasn't much to the L-shaped space. Just a small living area with a tiny adjoining kitchen. The common room encompassed a small rectangle holding one chair with fraying edges and a shabby couch losing stuffing from the corners. A coffee table littered with magazines and newspapers filled the drab environment. He couldn't believe four females lived here. Where was the ornamentation?

"Please have a seat." Charli's hands fluttered toward the couch—a painfully awkward move.

He grinned. She was uncertain with guests and trying not to show it. That characteristic would be adorable if her green eyes hadn't regarded him with suspicion and a tinge of fear. Hopefully he'd be able to erase all suspicion soon. After his interview with Chaunce, Felix had a good idea what was going on. And he was positive Miss Leighton was not a killer.

"Why don't *you* take a seat?"

She sank onto the couch, her look so lost he wanted to pull her into his arms again. That brief moment outside the club hadn't been enough, not nearly enough. The feel of her slender, warm frame against his had ignited a longing to touch her soft skin, to have those big, emerald eyes regard him with passion instead of mistrust. But that was a line he refused to cross. He was not a man to take advantage of a waif with no solid fortress.

He should leave, allow her some peace. But he wasn't ready for that. There must be something he could do to garner a small measure of her trust. Let her know he wasn't her enemy. He entered the adjoining kitchen, a room he crossed in three wide steps, and lifted the teakettle. "Do you have any coffee?"

She frowned, rubbing the back of her neck. "We're English. We drink tea." The long pause after she answered filled the short distance between them. She bit her lip. Was she considering being impolite, demand he leave? The fact she couldn't quite bring herself to say the words pleased him. He filled the kettle and put it on the burner, then ignited the flame.

"The tea leaves are in the cupboard over the stove. You'll find clean mugs on the counter." Her soft voice, low and throaty, pleased him even more. With those few words, he became an official guest.

While the kettle heated, he grabbed a towel and ran cold water over it, then returned to her. "Let's see what we can do to clean you up. You smell like a gin joint."

She grabbed the towel, wiping her arms and hands. "My tray was knocked away. I suppose most of my drinks landed on my dress."

She made a few futile swipes at her skirt before giving up. Her head fell in her hands. "I guess I'm out of work."

"Not to make too fine a point, but it wasn't that great of a job."

Miss Leighton lifted her chin, eyes flashing. "I can understand how you look down on the legality of it all. But there aren't many positions for people like me."

She was an enigma, a puzzle with delectable pieces he'd enjoy studying, learning more about. "Was marrying Hare so bad you would leave your wealthy lifestyle to live in a place like this?"

Her eyes hardened into shards of deep emerald, and her face flushed in fury. "I have higher aspirations than this." A second later her shoulders slumped. "How was I supposed to know the only thing I'm good at is considered a male profession?"

"I meant no disrespect." Felix kept his voice soft. His eyes fell to her lips...very appealing lips. What would it be like to kiss her? The kettle shrilled a most inopportune whistle. *Hell.* He darted back to the kitchen and prepared a cup for each of them.

Tea mugs in hand, he strolled back and sat, carefully leaving space between them. He held out a cup. "What kind of aspirations?"

She took the tea from him, staring into its golden depths without replying for several moments. Finally, she took a dainty sip and shrugged as if coming to a decision. "I came here to have my own bakery."

"What made you look to that vocation?"

Her face glowed with a fervor he'd not seen till now. Those enchanting green eyes bright with mirth. "When I was a child, I spent a great deal of time indoors. Mostly in the warmth of the kitchen. Our cook more or less took me under her wing, all the while grumbling about my being underfoot. She began teaching me to bake, and I was in paradise." She lifted her head and captured him with her luminous gaze.

"I'm quite good, you know. It's the only thing I love doing. I could quite literally spend the whole day baking."

His heart pounded, her excitement seeming to have transferred to him. Though, if he were honest, his excitement was for a much different reason. "Have you tried to get a job as a cook?"

She blew air through her bangs, glaring at him. "Of course. But I'm female."

"Oh, Right. I'm sorry."

Her gaze turned thoughtful. "However, I've met the owner of Carter department stores." Miss Leighton's eyes rounded with eagerness. "She wants to put a café in the center of the store. I baked scones for her." Her face fell. "But I've not seen her since I handed them over."

"Perhaps you'll hear from her soon." He lifted his cup to his lips. So Miss Leighton wanted to be a baker. As soon as this Hare business was done, she should have no problem pursuing the career of her choice. His thoughts drifted back to Chaunce. If Felix had unnerved the man enough, the weasel would make his move soon. If that damned raid hadn't botched things up. If they had waited a few more days, things would've been cleaner.

But with a little luck, they'd soon nail the bastard.

****

Where had that blasted Eliza disappeared to? She'd all but dragged Charli to the election party only to abandon her the minute they stepped inside the ballroom. What the devil was she supposed to do? Dance? Alone? Charli had never felt less like dancing. It didn't help that every time she was alone she thought about Detective Noble. A full day had passed with no sight of the man. He obviously suspected she was involved with Geoffrey's murder yet treated her with such tenderness, *compassion*. And those electric blue eyes filled her with a longing she didn't truly understand. She shook her head. It was all too confusing.

She traipsed around the edge of the Plaza Hotel's largest ballroom. Such luxury reminded her of home, even with its small circumference. The polished pink marble accented by gold trim along the walls. She couldn't deny the hotel staff's splendid job judging from the line of tables that held a mass of delectable items. Each table filled with specific food. She ran a finger over the edge of the buffet table where fragrances of stuffed pheasant, roast duck, and beef caused her stomach to rumble in a very unladylike fashion. She glanced around, relieved no one was near enough to hear the beastly noise. Side items were displayed on the next table, but Charli had her eye on the table just past. A three-tiered cake decorated in red, white, and blue was the centerpiece, surrounded by creampuffs, petit fours, and strawberries and cream. The variations were spectacular. So many, she couldn't make them all out. For a second, all thoughts of Geoffrey and the nightmare in which she resided fell away.

She circled to the front of the pastry table. Her mouth watered at the sight of such colorfully decorated cakes and cookies. Tasting each and every one of the pastries would be heaven but for the havoc life's recent events tossed in her lap like a bowl of salad greens. Her stomach growled at the sight of so much food. There was no way she'd be able to eat everything. Just a sampling, then. She lifted a plate, surveying the table.

"Miss Leighton, are you all right, my dear? I heard about the raid."

Charli whirled around to face the only person in the world she wanted to see more than Eliza. "Mrs. Carter, it's so good to see you. Yes, I'm fine. Perfectly fine." Before she could stop herself, she dipped into a small curtsey.

The shock on the woman's face sent a horrific flush of embarrassment through Charli.

"I-I'm sorry. I was just so excited to see you I guess I'd forgotten I wasn't home, um, England"

The woman's shock shifted to the dry amusement of motherly doting. "Miss. Leighton." She tipped Charli's chin up. "There is no need for that kind of pomp and circumstance with me."

Charli pressed her gloved hands against her cheeks. The coolness of cotton pulled the heat away. "I'm sorry."

Mrs. Carter dismissed the sentiment with a wave of her hand. "I've sampled those scones of yours, and they are quite the most divine thing I've ever had the fortune to taste."

"You did? They are?" Charli dropped her hands and clasped them behind her back to prevent wrapping the woman in a hug. She'd embarrassed herself enough for one evening. "I'm so glad."

Charli didn't wish to gush. She practically quivered waiting for Mrs. Carter to say more. But she seemed more concerned with loading her plate with petit fours. This couldn't be the end of the conversation. Maybe it was up to Charli to keep the conversation going. She needed just the right words. Ones that made her look professional but not desperate.

"Um…" That was not a good start. "Have you given any more thought to your café?"

Mrs. Carter nibbled a cake looking all the world like she was somewhere else. Charli was certain she hadn't sounded desperate. She frowned. Perhaps she'd been a bit abrupt. Had she ruined her chance? Then Mrs. Carter's eyes cleared and focused solely on Charli.

"Yes, that's why I'm so glad to have run into you here. I wasn't sure I'd see you again now that Club 501 has closed. I was hoping you would be available to discuss a position."

"Yes." Charli clamped her hands together to keep from bouncing up and down like a silly schoolgirl. "I would be happy to discuss a position with you."

"Excellent." Mrs. Carter held out her hand. Charli shook it. "How does 2:00 Monday afternoon at my store sound to you?"

"Perfect."

"Hello, Charli. Mrs. Carter." Charli flinched at the interruption. *Slick.*

Charli's spirits fell.

"Mr. Chaunce, what a delight." Mrs. Carter said in a tone that indicated the exact opposite. "If you'll excuse me. I shall see you on Monday, Miss Leighton."

Mrs. Carter sashayed away, and Charli sighed with relief. She hadn't canceled the meeting. All was good, for now. "Slick, what are you doing here?"

"Checking on you, as always."

"That isn't necessary."

"I'm not so sure. Your friend Noble and his partner paid me a visit."

Charli's hand flew to her breast, but nothing could stop the deep thumping of her heart. It seemed Slick made it his duty to ruin every good moment in her life. She couldn't even savor her victory because he kept mincing around. Accusing her of treachery. She said between closed teeth. "I haven't told them anything."

"How did they know to talk to me?"

"How am I supposed to know? I'm not the only one they questioned."

"How are you this evening, Miss Leighton?" A new but familiar baritone interrupted them. She turned her gaze into deep blue eyes. Recognition cleared her head, and her back went rigid. "What an unexpected surprise to see you here."

"Detective Noble, I would say the same to you." Charli favored him with a welcoming smile.

Slick scowled and tossed back his drink. He sniffed, shifting his gaze from Charli to Felix, eyes narrowed. Then he dipped his head briefly and slithered off in the other direction.

Felix's lips curved in an inviting smile. "A fan of Coolidge, are you?" No trace of the sternness touched him. Just something kind and warm. Like the other night when she'd confessed her deepest desire. She leaned her head to one side. What was he about? Had he followed her to further his investigation? Or was he a guest like her? No matter the reason, his nearness made her pulse race.

She glanced quickly around. No Eliza. But emerging from a nearby archway, she spotted Harry Dempsey, the man Meggie carried a torch for, stalk toward the bandleader. She hardly recognized him decked out in his black suit and stark white shirt. She spied Jess across the room. But just as Charli wracked her mind for something plausible to extricate herself, Mr. Markov, who Jess found hotsy-totsy, stepped forward and twirled her friend onto the dance floor.

"Um, Mr. Coolidge? I'm British, sir. It hardly matters how I would have voted, given half the chance." Charli met his gaze, stunned at how calmly she faced him. This man could crush her future, rob her of her freedom, yet she faced him now still hoping for the best. "I admit, however, I am an avid fan of democracy." Her voice came out somewhat dry, and she had an urge—the first in so many days—to laugh. Instead, she spoke softly. "I think it's grand that the American people have the right to choose—their leader—their life. I think it's important to have a say in how the country is run. More than that, a crime when one has the opportunity to lend one's voice and doesn't. Don't you?"

"Indeed I do." His smile broadened as if they shared a special secret. He stepped closer and held out a hand. "Dance with me?" The low words were part request part demand.

Her hand flew to her chest, the erratic thumping of her heart pounding against it. She gaped at him. Surely, he was jesting. Detectives did not dance with someone they suspected of...of...*murder*.

Yet just as shocking was the desire *to* dance with him. The world slipped into a bizarre reel that played in her head. The events that followed playing out in a slow-motion dream world—his hand rising, taking the plate she held, slowly, as though afraid if he moved too fast she might skitter off like a frightened rabbit. Long, elegant fingers clasped hers in a gentle squeeze, guiding her to an open space in the dance floor. Then she was in his arms. She couldn't bring herself to lift her gaze any higher than the strong shoulders beneath the brown suit—one much nicer than the one he'd worn the other night. She wanted to lean against his broad chest. Had, in fact, leaned against it.

Reality seeped in, similar to a dissipating fog. She bit her lip and pulled away, but with his hold, could only manage two steps back. "I'm sorry, I-I'm not much of a dancer."

"Please." he said.

Her eyes darted to the table. The sumptuous desserts no longer held her enthralled. A rush of heat flooded her cheeks as he guided her perfectly through the steps. His stride was strong, his hand confident as it led her this way and that. She spun through the steps, never feeling off balance. "You dance very well, Detective."

"Surprised?" He arched an eyebrow.

"A little." She averted her gaze, aware her comment could be construed as an insult. It wasn't her intent to offend him. Being this close to him was unnerving. Breaking the silence with words, any words, was better than acknowledging the heat radiating through her or the way his intense blue gaze heightened her senses enveloping her in a gauzy nest of pleasure. Surprised to hear him laugh, she lifted her face to stare up at him. His eyes shone with merriment. He wasn't offended at all.

"Not all of us born out of nobility are without training in the classical arts, my dear. My mother adored fine things and made sure I learned about them too."

"Oh. So you grew up wealthy?"

The gaiety faded, and his eyes clouded with bitterness. The tides of his emotions changed so quickly she didn't know what to do. One minute he was laughing, the next voicing displeasure. "Not precisely. My mother simply believed too much in the American dream."

"How so?" She bit her lip against her rude inquisitiveness. What was it about this man that caused her to behave in such a brash manner? She peered at him, attempting to assess his reaction. It was far from what she expected. He didn't grimace. His eyes didn't flash with anger. Although he continued to expertly guide her through the dance, his gaze had misted over as though focused on his distant past.

"My mother spent us into penury. Wasting her money on any classical training that would push me into higher social circles. Her ambitions for me were too much."

"I don't understand. Things seem to have turned out all right."

He nodded, slowly. "Yes. Yes, I believe they did…or will."

They slid into companionable silence as they spun around the room. The chandeliers glittered, sending electric warmth onto the satin and sequin gowns, bouncing off the hair of each guest. Charli was breathless taking in the richness of the evening. She didn't wish it to turn darker, but curiosity consumed her. "If I may be so bold, what happened with your mother?"

He gazed off into the distance. "We were poor for a long time. She'd put all her hopes on me. I thought I had to fix the situation." He hesitated so long she thought he wouldn't answer. He spoke in a low murmur, as if he was no longer speaking to her. "I stole gold candlesticks—from a church."

Charli gasped.

His head tilted to one side, a wry expression on his face. "It wasn't the smartest thing to do."

"What happened?"

"Of course, I was caught. I was terrified I would go to prison. But an older officer, Officer Riley, took pity on me, made sure I returned them. Forced me to confess my crimes." He gave a self-deprecating laugh. "Certainly worse than any maximum-security prison." He shrugged. "Riley kept close tabs after that."

"That was nice of him."

"Nice. Yes. I suppose it was. Anyway, after that, my mother's ambitions were no longer mine. I decided then and there that my job was to protect people's rights."

Knots formed in Charli's stomach. Felix Noble was a good man and much more complex than she would ever have believed. He knew what it was like to be in a tight spot, understood being given another chance. Could that mercy pass to her? It was too much to expect. He was a constable. His life's work was to catch and punish those who deserved it. And she was responsible for a murder. Much worse than pilfering candlesticks. Unexpected tears filled her eyes.

He cleared his throat. "So tell me, have you given more thought to your predicament?"

Her chin dropped to her chest. She wasn't certain if he was asking about the murder or her job situation. So she allowed her response to answer either inquiry. "No."

He placed a finger under her chin and brought her gaze back to him. "I know you're out of work now, but surely you've given some thought on what to do next."

His face brimmed with curiosity like he really was concerned for her. Wanted her to succeed.

"I spoke with Mrs. Carter."

"And?"

"She wants to meet with me."

"That sounds promising."

She gaged him carefully, not sure if there wasn't the tiniest notion of sarcasm. "Yes, it does. It is my greatest desire to manage her bakery."

The music stopped. He whirled her into a graceful end, bowing as grandly as any noble she'd met in her coming-out year. "I wish you luck in your endeavor, Miss Leighton."

Charli stammered a "Thank you for the dance" and rushed off to find Eliza, Jess, Megs. Anyone who didn't fix her with a gaze that sunk deep into her lonely and pathetic heart.

****

Felix left the party feeling more energized than when he'd entered. Miss Leighton was close to reaching her dreams. He was overjoyed. No. More than that. He was proud. It amazed him how in a few short days the woman had wormed her way into his thoughts. The urge to protect her grew stronger every day, along with the certainty Miss Leighton was too gentle a creature to kill anyone.

He exited the Plaza into the brisk night air. In spite of the late hour, he would head back to the precinct.

Find out what the raid had uncovered. He rounded the corner.

A strike of a match lit up Chaunce's face. He placed the flame to a cigarette, sucking in a deep lungful of smoke. Leaning with one foot against the brick wall, he held the butt sandwiched between his fingers taking no notice of Felix.

"Mr. Chaunce, why is it wherever Miss Leighton is, I also find you?"

"What, you jealous?" Chaunce turned a sharp look on him. The slimy bastard.

"I just don't believe in coincidences." Felix closed in. "Just the other day you said you barely know her, and then I find you in a deep conversation today. What am I to make of that?"

"Make of it what you want." Chaunce tossed aside the butt and peeled away from the wall. As he walked away, he threw over his shoulder, "I suspect things will be clearer soon."

Felix smiled. The weasel was way too sure of himself. Felix quickened his steps, buoyed with a certainty that the rat had tried to tip the scales in his favor. The last few blocks were excruciating. He had to know if he was correct. Had they found something in the raid? He'd barely made it to his desk when Mike plopped a box on top.

"Guess what our friends found?" the pleasure in Mike's voice was evident.

"As we suspected?" Felix opened the box.

"Just as we suspected."

Felix lifted a bloodstained apron from the box. Charlotte's name was stitched with precision on the inside of the sash. He examined the dress. The burgundy color made it hard to detect, but blood stained the hem. Shit. If he couldn't pin this on Slick, he'd have to arrest her. No matter how repugnant the thought, it was his job to do so.

"Where was it?"

"In the back room. Where Miss Leighton's personal effects were kept."

Felix's heart leapt. "And you're certain it wasn't there when you searched the place prior to the raid?"

"Absolutely."

"Then I guess I'd better find out what Miss Leighton has to say."

Chapter Seven

Charli swept through her small flat, humming, glad for these few moments alone. Last night's party had been full of fun and surprises. To top it all off, tomorrow she would meet with Mrs. Carter to discuss plans for her new bakery. She could hardly contain her excitement as she scurried around the kitchen. Readying herself to bake was no chore, especially now that she was realizing her dreams.

A sharp knock interrupted her thoughts. She opened the door and stopped short. Detective Noble stood before her. His handsome face was drawn, his mouth set in a grim line. Nothing like the man who'd twirled her about the dance floor or confided his reckless childhood. Just rigid and somber, hands holding a box stuffed with rags.

His ominous mood enveloped her, and her stomach dipped. She looked closer. No, not rags—her soiled clothes. She gasped.

"Miss Leighton." He strode through the door. "I executed a search warrant on your cupboard at Club 501. Imagine my surprise in finding these." He held out the box containing her blood-spattered apron and dress.

Her heart stilled. She shivered. "I-it's not what you think."

"Isn't it? Then suppose you enlighten me. They are covered in blood."

She searched his face, but no malice shadowed his features. Just business. Here to do his job. Her spirits fell. Did she see concern reflected in his blue eyes? Or was that just her imagination reaching for a reason to trust him? Her life was over. She had nowhere else to go. She was standing in her last refuge.

Tears spilled down her face and, her legs refusing to hold her, buckled. She crumpled to the floor, but the detective caught her elbow. He led her to the couch where she sank into the cushions. It was all over. Her dreams snatched away on the eve of being realized.

"You wouldn't understand," she whispered. It couldn't end this way. She hadn't killed Geoffrey. But she'd concealed it. Kept silent while the true killer went about free. Now Slick had boxed her in, and she had nowhere to run.

"Miss Leighton, you need to tell me what happened. I swear, you'll feel better." He held out his handkerchief. The way he did the first time they'd met. She wiped her eyes, gathering her fortitude.

Nothing to do now but confess. Everything. Something she should have done in the beginning. A horrific crime had been committed, and the guilty must pay, even if it meant losing her freedom. "I was leaving work." Her hands flailed as if grasping her words from the air. "Geoffrey found me and was trying to take me back to England. I refused. And, and…" She sniffed and wiped her nose.

"Yes," Felix leaned in and patted her shoulder. "You're doing fine. Go on."

"I was running for my flat, but Geoffrey caught me. He chastised me for being childish. While we were arguing, Slick showed up."

"Is he in the habit of following you?"

"No." She wiped her eyes. "I don't know what he was doing there. Then all of a sudden he had a knife and he…he…"

"What did he do, Miss Leighton?"

"He thrust it at Geoffrey." She hiccupped a sob. "There was so much blood. I told him we should call the constable, but he said I would be arrested." Her heart ached so hard it cut off her breath. She broke down crying and could say no more.

"Miss Leighton, you don't know how relieved I am to hear that." Felix pulled her from the chair and held her against his solid chest. Cocooned in a temporary haven, she leaned in, clinging to the spicy scent, a torrent of tears streaming down her face. How could he be so kind when he knew her worst deed? "We can fix this, but I need your help."

She stemmed the flow of tears and raised her face to his. "How can I help?"

"We need a confession from Mr. Chaunce. You need to get him to admit what happened where I can hear it."

****

Charli waited in the back room of Club 501. It was strange to be back in the establishment full of crushed glass and broken furniture. The room was in shambles when she'd gotten here with Felix. They'd had to right the table and chairs so she'd have a place to sit. How would she ever be able to convince Slick she'd found the apron on her own? She sat, ankles crossed, one foot tapping against the other. Felix hid in the janitor's closet. She chewed her thumbnail. An act for which her mother would've doused her fingers in castor oil and sent her to bed without supper. But her mother didn't know the fix she was in. Gnawing her thumbnail raw was a small grievance next to allowing a murderer to go free.

Slick should be here soon. She'd run through the plan with Felix several times, but she wasn't sure she could pull it off. Her legs trembled, and her hands shook. How could someone as unintimidating as her get Slick to confess? Of course she had to try. If she didn't, she'd go to prison for a murder she didn't commit.

Slick's voice filtered in from the hallway. "Charli, you here?"

"Yes," Charli said. "I'm in the back room."

Run! Please run! Felix's force was waiting in the alleyway if Slick attempted to flee. She wouldn't have to confront him then. If they caught him fleeing a meeting with her in the back room, she wouldn't have to deal with him. Her heart sank when he waltzed into the room.

"Hey, doll?"

She mustered all her courage as she rose from her chair. With a stiff back, she walked over to cupboard number nine. She reached into her cubby and shoved her bloody clothes into his view. "I found these in my cupboard. I thought you got rid of them."

Slick's face went blank. He wandered around the room with an easy, measured gait. But his narrowed eyes were alert, scanning every inch of the room. Had he guessed at their intentions? He stopped before her cupboard. "Got rid of what?"

"Don't play dumb with me. You promised you'd take care of this."

"You've got the wrong guy, doll." He shook his head. "Someone might have put them here, but it wasn't me."

"Yes it was."

He wandered back in her direction, tracing a finger along the doors. "Don't know anything about them."

"Yes you do. I gave them to you."

"Look, doll," Slick shrugged. "Whatever you've gotten yourself into has nothing to do with me."

"You can't be serious." She swallowed. A cold stone slid down her throat and settled in her stomach. Fighting the urge to retch, she stood and stumbled toward him, bloody apron outstretched. "You put this here after you murdered Geoffrey."

"That's the trouble with my lot." He huffed and looked toward the ceiling. Hands firmly stuffed in his pockets. "Everybody trying to lay one on me."

"What are you talking about?" Charli stared at his innocent act, mouth open. This couldn't be happening. He was denying his involvement, and she had no proof other than her own words. She shut her eyes. She'd never anticipated denial. Anger. Yes. Violence. Yes. But not this calm person shrugging off her accusations.

"Look." He leveled a wicked gaze on her. One full of mocking venom. But that was all for her. Felix couldn't see the shrewdness in his eyes. The rest of his face was relaxed and worry free. "I'm not sure what you're playing at here. I want no part of it."

He stalked toward the door. He was leaving. In a few brief seconds it would all be over, and she'd be left drinking from a dirty glass. Her vision dimmed, filling the space with blackness. She stumbled back, holding onto the chair to keep from falling. She had to find the words that would get him to speak the truth. Something he didn't do as a habit. But a little dose of honesty could go a long way. "You call yourself a gentleman. Is this how a gentleman acts? Throwing a lady to the wolves? I thought you were trying to protect me."

He swiveled toward her, his back stiff and unrepentant. "I am a gentleman, love."

"Oh that's right," Charli didn't recognize her voice. It was loud, clear, and full of confidence. "You're such a gentleman you'd pin a murder on an innocent woman."

Slick frowned wiping the back of his neck. "You're not so innocent."

Slick shook his head like he was trying to rid himself of sticky goo. His voice was less certain now. Encouraged, Charli continued. "I never asked you to kill Geoffrey."

"No." Slick pointed his finger at her. "But you wanted to get away from him. That's motive enough, and you're the one with blood on your clothes." He waved her off. "I'm not responsible for your stupidity or clumsiness.'

"I'm stupid and clumsy am I?" She rounded him. He blinked rapidly while he took a step back. *Off your guard?* "I'm going to tell the constables everything. And *they're* going to believe me."

"You've got nothing on me."

"Truly? No one believes I have the strength to shove a knife into a man's gut. I don't even own that kind of knife."

Slick's mouth pulled taut, white tinging the edges. He said nothing, but he didn't move either. His cold eyes never wavered from her. Now was her chance. She held his gaze, pulling the bloody clothes to her bosom, and walked past him.

He grabbed her arm and tugged her back. "Where are you going?"

"To the constables."

"You ungrateful bitch." He pushed her against the wall. "I did nothing but try to help you."

"You did nothing but help yourself," she bit out. He wrapped his fingers around her neck and squeezed. His thumb and index finger dug into her flesh sending tendrils of pain through the base of her neck. She attempted to inhale but no air filtered through.

"I killed Hare for you, and all you can do is insult me?"

Charli clawed at his hand but couldn't wrench it free. Dizziness descended, and the world dimmed. Then Felix was there looming behind Slick. He grabbed Slick's shoulder and ripped him away. Felix slammed his fist into Slick's jaw. Charli brought her hands to her throat and inhaled big gulps of air as her body slid to the floor. Felix flipped Slick onto his stomach and snapped handcuffs on him. "Derrick Chaunce, you're under arrest for murder."

Slick wrenched his head until his wide eyes lit on Charli. "No, she's the one. I was only trying to help her."

"Bullshit. I heard it all. Now you're going to rot in prison."

Two uniformed officers entered the room and jerked Slick to his feet. They pushed him against the wall, pinning his arms behind him. Slick struggled against their hold, eyes bulging. He howled. "You've got the wrong person. Charli wanted him dead. He was trying to take her back to England."

"Enough!" one of the officers said. As they pushed him out the door, Slick looked at Charli. "You're just as guilty as me. This isn't over."

Felix knelt next to Charli. "Are you okay?"

She flung herself into his arms. "Thank you for saving me."

He chuckled and rubbed a hand soothingly down her back. "You're welcome. Maybe next time you'll think twice before you distrust a police officer."

Epilogue

"Congratulations to Meggie and Harry." Jess saluted the happy couple with a fluted glass of champagne. "May you find much happiness."

Charli lifted her glass in unison with the other guests. Meggie was an exceptionally beautiful bride in a white flowing gown that accentuated her voluptuous curves. Her blonde locks draped her shoulders, head adorned only with a diamond tiara. Harry, dressed in a tuxedo, smiled down at his songbird bride.

Charli smoothed her hands over her rose-colored dress. Its iridescent crystal beads sparkled under the chandeliers. It was nice to be wearing fashionable clothes again rather than that cocktail frock, but better than both was the baker's jacket she donned daily for her position at the café. So much had happened since she, Jess, Meggie, and Eliza had boarded the *Empress of India* in search of their dreams.

All four had accomplished what they'd set out to do. Jess was happily married to Frank. Eliza was there with her beau, the former prizefighter Vince Taggart, who had been trying for months to convince her to marry him and move to his home in Philadelphia. Eliza was a stubborn cuss, but Charli was certain she was close to giving in—there was no doubt she was over the moon in love with him. All had turned out for her friends.

"Will we be that happy?" Felix whispered in her ear, sending pleasant shivers down her back.

"Happier." She laced her fingers through his, eyeing the diamond ring on her finger. It didn't seem real somehow, standing beside the man who would be her husband. But it was the most wonderful feeling in the world.

"All unattached Janes gather in the center. It's time for the bride to toss her bouquet."

"I think that means you." Felix winked.

Charli crowded in with the others. It was almost like cheating since she was already engaged. But the rules weren't that specific. All the ladies twittered with anticipation as Meggie turned her back and tossed her bouquet. Charli reached up. The flowers landed in her grasp as if Meggie had planned it.

Charli strode toward Felix, a wide grin on her face. "I guess I'm next."

"Yes, you are." His arms encircled her, one hand at the small of her back urging her closer. He claimed her lips, sending flame-tipped spirals to her most private places. Her knees went weak. They'd better be next. She wasn't sure she could wait any longer for their life together to begin.

Martini Club 4: The 1940s

Priceless

Prologue

Martha's Vineyard, Summer 1937

"Come on, Sophie, I thought we were playing croquet." Audra called from across the lawn. She stood, stamping her foot, her face screwed up with impatience.

"I'll be there in a minute." Sophie Noble smiled as sweetly as possible. "I just need to finish this drawing."

School was out. The tedium and monotony of the same old routine was over. Summer was finally here, promising new adventures and delightful diversions with her childhood friends. A cool breeze tickled her nose. She breathed in the scent of summer sweet. The flowers' fragrant perfume hinting some grand adventure lay ahead. Maybe at the theater tonight. Her fingers slipped at the thought, leaving a pencil scar on one of the delicate petals she was shading. Shaking her head, she rubbed the mark out with a gum eraser. Best not to look too far into the future and concentrate on the here and now.

She shifted her seat on the stone ledge to get a better view of her subject. The garden was absolutely spectacular. The orange glory was in full bloom. Butterflies flitted between the small blossoms, their graceful wings fluttering from one tiny perch to another. The white structure of the house their families had rented set off the tiny star-shaped blossoms to perfection. It was too beautiful to ignore, and she had to capture it. This was the best subject she'd found so far to test out her new colored pencil set. As much as she loved New York City, there was a charm in Martha's Vineyard that couldn't be captured in her home town. It was quaint. Less crowded, blanketed with meadows filled with unspeakable loveliness.

"No, you need to join us now. We only have a few more hours of daylight. If we don't begin immediately, none of us will have time to get ready for the play tonight."

"Hey can I help?" Sophie's brother Nathan flew across the yard to where Maddie and Iris were busy setting up the wickets in a figure eight formation. Maddie looked up at Nathan's approach and favored him with a doting smile, like he was a long-lost cousin rather than the knight in shining armor he wanted to be. Sophie sighed. Nate just didn't understand the age difference mattered. No matter how often he was told, he ignored the gentle warning and mooned after Maddie anyhow.

The trio continued to set up the croquet course. No one paid attention to Audra's glowering disapproval at Sophie's lack of participation. Most of the time, she loved spending the summer with Maddie, Audra, and Iris. But right now all she wanted was a bit of solitude to complete her new masterpiece. Never mind that she had promised to play the game just moments ago. That was before she spotted the garden at the side of the house. It wasn't like it was a surprise her art supplies went with her everywhere. Audra knew she drew when the muse struck.

"But the lighting is perfect for my picture. It will only take a few minutes, I swear." She went back to her drawing that didn't come near to capturing the brilliance of the plant. Retrieving another pencil, she outlined the orange petal with dark crimson. Dotting the star points of each tiny flower. The color, bright and vibrant, contrasted by the stark white of the house.

"And what is it that is so important that you can't spare a moment for your friends?" Audra loomed over her, casting dark shadows over the masterpiece. She turned the drawing around to her perspective. "Flowers? That's what has you so preoccupied?"

Audra yanked the picture from Sophie's lap, toppling her portfolio to the lawn. A gust of wind blew past. The artwork recently pinned between its folds fluttered around the yard. Tumbling in the wind to the edges of the yard.

"My pictures." Sophie leapt to grab them before they got too far away. Iris and Maddie plucked up the papers that had gotten too far from Sophie's grasp. Nate raced around the yard retrieving papers that had drifted to the far end of the yard, handing them over to Maddie. His face beamed with pride with every nod of Maddie's head or softly spoken thank you. Sophie shook her head. When would Nate come to his senses? Maddie shuffled the errant pages together into a stack and walked toward Sophie, flipping through each one as she did.

"These are really good, Sophie." Maddie flipped through the pictures and pulled one out, scrutinizing it. "What's this?"

"Who cares? I thought we were going to play croquet." Audra threw up her hands, but even her aggravation didn't keep her eyes from traveling to the picture Maddie held in her hands. Audra let out a bark of laughter, yanking the picture away from Maddie. "Iris, you've got to come see this."

"Huh?" Iris straightened from her bent position gathering up the last of the papers. She clasped her pile close to her chest and made her way toward the small group huddling over the picture. Hopefully she hadn't picked up the charcoal drawings. Otherwise her dress was in for a huge sooty stain. Luckily she was wearing play clothes like Maddie and Sophie. Only Audra stood out in crisp white ruffles. It didn't matter how many times she'd returned with grass stains or dirt caking her black patent shoes, her mother required Audra always dress to fashion, her soft curls kept in check with a pink headband.

Iris handed her pile to Sophie. Sophie's heart sank at a black spot covering Iris's collar. But Iris didn't seem to notice the blemish or the charcoal coating her fingertips. She leaned over to view the picture that held Maddie and Audra captive. Iris grimaced. "It looks like a troll."

"It does." Maddie agreed. "Wait a moment. The face looks a lot like Nate."

"What?" Sophie shrieked and grabbed the picture out of Audra's grasp. It slid into full view. The caricature she'd drawn of Nate when she was cross. His form bent over with his shoulder blades sticking out like two rocks in a stream. His back covered with blotches and his talon-shaped fingers reaching to scratch his back. "You guys aren't supposed to see this."

"It's a little late now." Maddie said. "It's not the most flattering picture, is it?"

"No," Iris agreed. "It's not very nice either."

"Well, it wasn't meant for your eyes." Sophie moved to shove the picture back where it belonged, hidden from the public. Small, thin fingers grabbed it before it reached its safe haven. Sophie looked up to see who had snatched the picture this time. Nate stood ramrod straight. His mouth was drawn tight. Red tinged his cheeks.

"What is this?" Although he sniffed, the accusation hit dead on. His hands shook as he crumpled the paper. His watery brown eyes glared at me. "How dare you." Then he spun around. "Mooom!" He pushed through Iris and Audra carrying the damning evidence with him.

"Oh no." Sophie's hands flew to her cheeks, which were sure to be as crimson as her colored pencil. She was in for it now. Iris, Maddie, and Audra stood there gawking at her like horns had sprouted from her head. Audra with her hands on her hips. Iris shaking her head. Maddie biting her lip. "Don't judge me. You have no idea what a devil Nate can be."

Maddie arched her brow. "Perhaps. But public humiliation is never a good idea."

"It was an accident. I never meant for anyone to see it." Sophie threw up her hand. How was she supposed to predict her pictures would spill all over the ground?

"Sophie." Her mother's high-pitched voice sailed through the open window. "Get in here now."

The girls, traitors that they were, smiled and shrugged. All three trailed off to the croquet game. Gritting her teeth, Sophie trudged into the house to her doom. Her mother was going to be upset because her little prince was crying. Still, Sophie hadn't upset him on purpose. That had to count for something.

She entered the drawing room decorated in green and gold. Her mother was already perched primly on the sofa clutching the crumpled drawing. Her green eyes filled with shadows of disappointment. Sophie sunk into the chair across from her, not being able to bring herself to sit next to her. This would be no cozy tet-a-tet.

"Sophie, how many times do I need to tell you to be careful what you draw?"

"I drew that when I was mad at him." Sophie crossed her arms and sunk down into the cushion. "I didn't intend for anyone to see it."

"That doesn't matter." She folded the paper, clasping her hands together. "Art isn't meant to take revenge, sweetie."

"Sometimes it is." Like when her brother got into her things and ruined them.

"Sophie, I haven't raised you to be cruel. And this—" She held up the drawing, her hand shaking with effort. "—is just plain mean."

"Nate glued my hairbrush and mirror to my nightstand." Sophie huffed. "That wasn't nice either."

"And he was taken to task for it." Although mother's hands rested calmly in her lap, her lecture was far from over. She never really yelled at her children. The look of dark disappointment was bad enough. "Two wrongs don't make a right."

Sophie scoffed, balling her hands into fists. "It took weeks to undo that. Nate isn't the angel you think he is."

"You created an embarrassing time for Nate. He suffered terribly when it was discovered he was allergic to chocolate. He almost scraped himself raw because the hives itched so much. And you memorialized it here." She held up the picture, its crumpled form unraveling in her hand. "Until you can use your art for more useful purposes, I'm taking away your colored pencils. "

"That's not fair." Sophie pounded on the arms of the chair. "Nate makes it impossible for me to use my things, and all he gets is a slap on the wrist. And you're taking away my reason for living all because of an accident."

Her mother glowered at her. "It was more than that, and you know it."

"No, it wasn't." Honestly, how could her mother blow this so out of proportion? Nate was probably already over it.

"Be that as it may, I am disappointed that you show no remorse for this act. I have no choice but to leave you at home tonight. You will not be attending the play."

"What?" Sophie leapt from her chair. "You can't do that. The tickets have already been purchased. That's a waste of money."

"Nate will attend in your place." She said it so calmly, like she was announcing all they had was peanut butter and jelly for lunch.

"He doesn't even want to see the play." Her vision blurred. Tears threatened to spill down her face. She looked up at the ceiling, not wanting her mother to see them.

"It will be good for him to get some culture, and you need to learn some manners."

"You're being way too harsh."

Her mother stood, hands braced against her hips. "That's enough lip from you, young lady. If your behavior doesn't improve, I will have no alternative but to cancel your private art lessons with Mrs. Blanchard."

Before she would say something she would regret, Sophie spun on her heels and stomped up the stairs. She didn't stop until she reached the room she shared with Iris, Audra, and Maddie. She sniffed, wiping the tears from her eyes. Really, her mother was making too much over one stupid drawing. She flung herself on the bed, allowing the tears full reign. Tonight she would be trapped in this drafty old house while everyone else, include her silly brother, was out having fun. Her mother, the baker, thought she was an art critic. She didn't know the first thing about what it took to be a real artist.

For a long time Sophie lay on her back staring at the cracked white ceiling. What a dreary sight. Unable to help herself, she imagined painting fluffy clouds with cheerful golden birds soaring in an aqua blue sky. She'd never get a chance to paint something like that now that her mother had taken her art supplies away. All she'd done was express her feelings on paper. Until it was discovered, it had only served to sooth her bruised ego. From her mother's reaction that was one big no-no. So from this day forward she wouldn't put one negative thing into her creations. If she only painted pretty, happy things she wouldn't get into trouble. Feeling a little better, she closed her eyes and fell asleep.

Chapter One

Boston, Monday, May 12, 1947

"Thank you all for consenting to this impromptu excursion." Sophie couldn't believe she talked the girls into going to the MET. Well, Maddie was an easy sell. She was just as into art as Sophie was. But it was a real coup that Audra and Iris were willing to traipse along. "I've wanted to see the *Rape of the Sabine Woman* since I heard it was on display here."

The painting sounded so naughty even though she knew it was about abducting women for wives rather than the more vile interpretation of the title. Still, the subject matter was so intriguing it had been painted by multiple artists. This one by Poussin surely wouldn't disappoint her. She dashed up the steps, anxious to see the newly acquired painting.

"No need to rush, Sophie," Audra said, making her stately way up the stairs. "The painting is here for weeks."

"True, but I'm just so excited I'm actually going to see it." Sophie didn't slow her pace. Seeing a painting of this magnitude was too important.

"The next thing we know she'll be sliding down the banisters," Audra whispered to Iris.

"That would not surprise me," Iris whispered back, her steps matching Audra's pace exactly. Sophie shook her head. Iris wanted so badly to be part of the upper crust. Sophie had no idea why. Too many restrictions on comportment and behavior. Chains no matter how golden were still chains. Freedom was so much better than that.

Sophie had broadened the distance between the two negative Nancy's by the time she'd reached the designated floor. Maddie, she was pleased to see, was keeping pace with her. The minute the painting came into view Sophie was entranced. Every brush stroke and hue had been chosen to evoke the chaos and terror as the Romans carried off the women by force. Each woman garbed in blue or gray while the Roman soldiers wore unyielding steel armor. Their leaders were robed in authoritarian gold or red directing their troops. Men toppled trying to protect their women. Two children cried on the ground as their mother was carried off. Beneath a turbulent ashen sky, the buildings and columns shadowed in a dark brown cast.

"How ghastly." Audra drew up beside Sophie and took in the painting with wide eyes. "They must have been terrified."

"I couldn't imagine." Iris covered her mouth equally as shocked at the carnage.

"It's beautiful." The words were out of Sophie's mouth before she could contain them. Maddie smiled but said nothing. Audra and Iris looked at her with disapproval. "What? Just because the subject is a terrible event doesn't mean I can't appreciate the work of art. Look at the way the artists bring out the fear of the villagers, the pleading nature of the women, and the cold indifference of the soldiers. It's fantastic."

"Really, Sophie," Audra said. "Sometimes I worry about you."

A slow burn crept up her cheeks. Sophie opened her mouth to say something. Anything. But closed it just as quickly. She sighed. The only one who could understand her appreciation was Maddie, and she had wandered off to gaze at the other portraits in the immense gallery. Sophie turned away from Audra's and Iris's scrutiny, no longer happy they had come along. She shook off the gloom that had descended like a lead weight on her shoulders and took off in another direction.

The portraits blurred as Sophie walked past them. None of them covered even a hint of the raw desperation in the *Sabine* painting. Many depicted the birth of the Christ child. Mother Mary with a halo around her head. The crucifixion. Squaring her shoulders, she headed into the next gallery where the subject matter contained more than religious content. A male figure bent over a painting of a still life. Examining every nuance of the grapes and oranges. As she drew nearer, she stopped short. It was Professor Ray Critchton, the dean of the art department at Roseline's college. From what she'd heard none of the older art faculty was happy he'd replaced old Umberland after his death. Professor Critchton was selected over many more deserving candidates. One of them her favorite art professor.

Sophie turned at a right angle and went the other direction. Professor Critchton was the last man she wanted to see. Always looking down his nose at her. Shaking his head and tsking as if she'd done something wrong. She couldn't figure out why. Professor Overton raved about her talent as an artist. Always offering up her pieces as examples of good art. Surely, Professor

Critchton was aware of that. Faculty talked about their students, didn't they? Besides, Professor Critchton made rounds every now and then and had actually seen some of her work. But he never seemed impressed.

What always startled her was that he was so young. He couldn't be more than thirty-five. Professor Overton was way older than that. Critchton was slim with broad shoulders. His dark, brooding eyes always sending her a quiver. Why did he have to be as attractive as he was annoying? He never smiled but had a pleasant enough face when he looked at her head-on rather than down his nose. That was practically never.

Whatever she had done to vex him was a huge mystery. No chance to fix it, but there was seldom a need as their paths rarely crossed. Until now. She glanced over her shoulder as she left the gallery. He'd moved on to another painting. There was something endearing about his attention to every nuance and detail. He'd never looked at one of her paintings like that. Maybe he thought she had no talent. The thought left her so hollow it surprised her. It wasn't as though the man should be important to her.

She rushed through the gallery and pushed into the next. This gallery was more like it. Empty. She drew in a deep breath. It was always better to enjoy art by oneself. She took her time gazing at the paintings. It was the impressionist's wing. Her favorite art era. Fields of poppies, haystacks, and rural images. So picturesque and colorful.

Then a painting stopped her short. She knew every brush stroke. Every choice of color. Each placement of the flowers and chairs. She read the information plate. It had been donated from the Menard family collection.

But that couldn't be right. The painting had been created by her only a few weeks ago. Her body went stiff and cold. This had to be a mistake. She shook her head to clear it and read the information again. This couldn't be. She painted this work in art class. How in God's name had it gotten here being pawned off as a Van Gough no less? This wasn't possible. Just to be sure she checked the signature. It was a spot-on match for the artist's signature but just below it was the Celtic symbol of four friends. Her symbol. Her indication the painting was a fake.

"Enjoying the new Van Gough?" A rich baritone voice spoke behind her. She looked over her shoulder. Of course it was him. This day couldn't get any worse.

"I am indeed, Professor Critchton." She tried to sound nonchalantb but her voice hitched at the endb evoking a smooth smile from the odious man. He stepped beside her scrutinizing the painting.

"It's an interesting piece to be sure."

"How so?" Her voice had yet to calm down. She clasped her hands behind hcr back to keep them from shakingb but her knees quivered. Hopefully not enough to be noticed.

"It's a very good use of color and contour."

"Oh," She almost audibly sighed in relief. He hadn't discovered the painting was a forgery. Which he should have since he was an art expert. Maybe he had and didn't want to alert her to the fact. What business could it be of hers anyway? Unless he had seen this work in class, there was no way for him to know it was her painting on the wall.

He gazed at Sophie, scrutinizing her almost as intensely as he did the paintings. "I'm glad to see you taking in great works of art, Miss Noble. It's time you take art seriously."

She almost issued a most unladylike snort. "I've always taken my art seriously."

"Drawing caricatures is hardly serious art."

She quelled the urge to spit in his eye. It would be unseemly not to mention an act of insubordination. But just how was she to take this comment. She shifted uneasily carefully crafting a response. "I create more than caricatures, you know."

Instead of sounding suave and controlled it came out sounding petulant and spoiled. She couldn't have looked more childish if she had stomped her foot at him. She swallowed, her mouth suddenly dry. How could such a skinny twig intimidate her this much? Of course it could be more his position at the school than the man in front of her that was so unnerving.

"Good. Our students should graduate well rounded."

She had no idea how to respond to that statement. The pretentious bastard. Who appointed him lord of worthy art anyway? Thank goodness she graduated in less than a week. She would never have to see him again. They stood for a few awkward seconds. Professor Critchton looking down his nose at her, Sophie rooted to the spot. Then he bowed, a slow smile curving his lips. "Have a good rest of the afternoon, Miss Noble."

"Thank you." She took that moment to dash out of the hall into the ladies' lounge. She sunk into an overly stuffed chair. How did her painting get to the MET? More importantly, what was she going to do about it?

****

She rushed down the hall of the art department heedless of the impropriety. It was important to address the issue of how her painting had mysteriously appeared in the MET. The only one who could shed light on her dilemma was Professor Overton. Her teacher and mentor during her undergraduate years at Roseline College. As she reached the doorway to his office, a woman nearly bowled Sophie over.

"Pardon me," she said clutching her gloved hands to her chest. A small reticule dangling from her left arm. Her red rimmed eyes looked at Sophie with sorrow and something more.

"Are you all right?" It didn't seem like she was. Her arms trembled, and she looked like she was on edge. Had the professor threatened a failing grade? Sophie didn't recognize her. She must be from a newer class.

"Yes." She turned to walk away. As if as an afterthought she said over her shoulder. "Be careful."

Now what did she mean by that? Sophie didn't have the time to mull over that puzzle. She had a dire situation of her own to attend to. Sophie breezed into Professor Overton's office, uncertain of her next move. The professor stood with his back to her, gazing out the window. She waited a few minutes. He didn't move. She cleared her throat. He jumped and turned. "Oh, Miss Noble, I didn't hear you come in. What can I do for you?"

He sat at his desk, not looking in command of himself. He was distracted somehow. Her thoughts returned to the young woman who had left moments ago. What was that about? She was tempted to broach the subject, but that would be rude. It wasn't her business. However, if she chanced upon the lady again, she would certainly inquire as to her wellbeing. But right now she had to focus on the issue of her painting.

"I have a problem." She wasn't sure how to phrase it. She didn't want to sully the name of the college. Nor did she want to insult her professor, who'd been nothing but kind to her. But someone had gotten hold of her class project and used it for a nefarious purpose. Sophie shuddered. Who would have done such a thing?

"What kind of problem?" His ruddy cheeks stiffened over his clasped hands. Although the question was pointed at her, his eyes had a far-off look as if he was focused on something different than her.

"Remember that Van Gough I painted in our class on impressionism?"

"Yes." Still not paying attention to her.

"I saw it hanging in the MET. And it was being passed off as an original."

"Pardon me?" His ice blue eyes snapped to her. Now she had his attention. His face whitened. "Are you sure?"

"Of course I'm sure. I know my own work. What I want to know is how it got there?"

"I'm sure I have no idea." He rubbed his eyes. "You do good work but not good enough to hang in a museum."

Was he daft? "You misunderstand me. The painting was being passed off as a real Van Gough."

"That's not possible." He grimaced. "Museums are very careful about the pieces they put in their galleries. As good as your work is, it is hard to believe it can be passed off as genuine."

"I had the same thought, but I'm not seeing things. The painting is there." Sophie looked at the ceiling. Its taupe color not soothing but mocking. Did he think she was thinking too highly of herself? That her ego had gotten in the way of reality? There was only one way prove to him what she said was true. "Let's go take a look. All my projects are in my stall in the catacombs. I can show you the piece is missing."

"I'll tell you what." He put up a staying hand. "I'll look into the matter. It should be a simple matter of combing the catacombs to see what is missing."

That was more like it. At least now she was being taken seriously. "I'll go with you."

He stood. "Miss Noble, you're getting ready to graduate. There is no need to waste more time on it than necessary. Go out and enjoy yourself. I'll take care of this, I promise."

"You're sure?" She inhaled a deep breath of relief.

"Yes. Don't wish more trouble on yourself. I want you to graduate. Don't worry about this. I can handle it."

Sophie flinched and squinted at him as if the sun was in her eyes. His terse attitude was confusing. Was he threatening her? No. That was silly. He had no reason to threaten. But just to be sure. "Sir, I don't understand your meaning."

"I just don't want you to fret, that's all." He offered her a wide smile. "Graduation is an important accomplishment. You have parties to attend. It's your time to celebrate. Don't borrow trouble when you don't need to."

Still uncertain but too tired to argue, she left.

****

From her view on the side of the quadrangle, the garden party was in full swing. Groups of girls stood in groups chatting and sipping punch. Their parents sat at the tables watching their offspring with pride. No doubt comparing notes with each other. Sophie smoothed her hand over her ruby-red lace tea length dress. She loved the way it tapered at her waist and flounced out over her hips. If only her palms weren't so sweaty. Well there was nothing she could do about that. This was the afternoon she had waited for with both anticipation and dread. In moments she would pull off one of her best pranks ever. Everyone would really be celebrating then.

She located her mother, father, brother, and grandmama waiting for her at a table.

"It's about time you showed up." Grandmama glowered at Sophie. "It isn't polite to be late for a celebration being held in your honor."

"Really, Grandmama, haven't you heard of fashionably late." As disrespectful as she was being, Sophie didn't have it in her to back down. Her grandmother could suck the joy out of anything. This gathering was held to honor her graduating class, and Sophie was going to enjoy every minute of it.

"That's enough of your cheek, young lady." Her grandmother raised one gnarled hand, jabbing a pointy finger at her.

"Now, now mother." Sophie's mother placed her hand over her mother's. "Sophie is here now, and doesn't she look beautiful?"

Grandmother sniffed and nodded curtly. Bravo, Mother. Sophie was certain to get a lecture later when the public wasn't around. Her mother would do nothing to stop the tirade then. But for now she would take the reprieve. Sophie made her way, hugging first her grandmother, then her mother, and finally her father.

"You look lovely, darling." Her father kissed her cheek. "I'm so proud of you."

"Thank you, Daddy." Sophie smiled, basking in his approval.

Nate walked up to them, craning his head around as if looking for someone. "Is Maddie here?"

"Of course, silly. I think I saw here over there standing by Aunt Jessie." Sophie pointed in the direction she thought Maddie was. Nate tore off in the direction she indicated. Some things just never changed.

"Sweetie, it's impolite to point."

"Sorry, Mother." Sophie quickly lowered her arm and tried to appear nonchalant.

"Do you have everything?" Mother's soft green eyes darted to the top of her head. "Where's your hat, dear? Tell me you didn't leave it in the car or hotel room."

"Relax, mother, it's right here." She lifted her hand holding the hat.

"Here, let me help you put it on." She took the hat and placed it on her head. "Do you need bobby pins?"

"Got them right here."

Her mother took them and worked them into the hat as if she were solving a puzzle. Once done, she stood back and contemplated her work. Sophie dared not move fearing the cap would topple from her head. "There. Better?"

Not really, but what else where there to say but, "Thanks, Mom."

She hugged her. "I'm so proud of you."

"I know."

When her mother moved away, her father took her place. His brown eyes shimmered with unshed tears. "My little girl is all grown up."

"Daddy." Sophie almost rolled her eyes but remembered not to be rude. This was part of the ritual after all. The fawning. The congratulations. This week marked her exit from childhood into full-fledged adulthood. Her parents were entitled to their tears. Their muttered congratulations. Their fond memories of their baby girl. But it was getting a bit suffocating.

From over her father's shoulder, her grandmother said, "Remember our agreement, child."

Sophie nodded. That was the problem. She needed to get a job fast. If she didn't her parents would whisk her off to her grandmamma to find a good match. Something about needing her to fall in line. Where that came from she didn't know. But it wasn't something she was going to seriously entertain. Her youth should be fun. Once shackled, there would be no more fun. She was certain of that. Hopefully, in a matter of days her grandmama's ultimatum would not be an issue. "I remember, Grandmama."

There was a slight tug on her arm. Her friend Peter stepped into her line of sight. "Sophie, you look wonderful."

"Thank you. Is everything ready?"

"You won't be disappointed. I'll be over at the south end of the quadrangle. See you soon. "He winked and then took off.

"That was odd. I wonder what that was all about." Her mother's eyes followed Peter as he made his way through the crowd.

"That's my friend Peter. He's helping me with a project." Sophie did her best to sound casual. Her mother's eyes narrowed anyhow. Sophie smoothed her skirt, acting like nothing was amiss.

"What are you up to ,dear?" Her mother placed a steady hand on Sophie's shoulder.

"Nothing, Mother." Sophie looked around the gaggle of girls chatting and gossiping with each other. Their smiles and giggles lifted her spirits. "I'm going to go see if I can find the girls."

Her mother eyed her suspiciously but finally nodded. "We'll be right here. Have a good time."

Left to her own devices she headed for the area Peter had indicated. She made her way through her classmates nodding and smiling as she passed. Excitement bubbled through her veins followed by incipient dread. She shook it off. This was her day, and she was entitled to enjoy it. Besides, she had a surprise brewing. It was going to be a great day.

Her grandmama would not win. Sophie would make the most of her youth. She would perfect her art. If that meant she would continue to freelance caricatures, so be it. Political art and satire had its place no matter what Professor Critchton thought. No. She would not let his dour opinion of her intrude on her day. Everyone had to start somewhere. Buoyed by that thought she made her way toward Peter.

Away from the crush of party attendees Peter stood with the small load of contraband that would be sure to cause a stir. As Sophie approached, Peter's face broke out in a wide grin. He motioned her forward with a flick of his hand. Sophie could barely contain herself. This would be by far the best prank she would ever pull off.

"Are you sure they'll work?" Her voice positively squeaked with excitement.

"Of course I'm sure. My father taught me how to set off fireworks. "

Peter pulled out a cone and held it up as if it was a prized Monet. Sophie couldn't disagree with this notion. The display would be a work of art no matter how ephemeral. Then he set about the work of placing seven cones in a row. Using a lighter, he lit each fuse. She held her breath as the flames eagerly ate its way to its destination.

As each one hit, the sky erupted in a spectacular display of color. Sophie stood awestruck as they dipped toward the ground sparkling with green, reds, and golden streaks. They blossomed and crackled with authority.

"Oooh!" She clapped her hands together and squealed. This was better than she had imagined. "Let me try."

Peter frowned. "I'm not sure that's a good idea. You haven't been trained."

"Good grief. How hard can it be to light a fuse?" She grabbed the lighter from his hand and pulled another cone out of the box. She walked to the demolished cones and placed it next to them.

Peter followed her like a wounded puppy. "All right, but you have to follow my instructions."

"Oh, I will." This was even better than she'd planned. She was going to get to set the sky on fire.

He straightened out the fuse and led her to the end of it. Just as she bent to light the fuse, a thud of footsteps halted her progress. He stood behind her much closer than she liked and guided her hand to the fuse. "Ok, the minute you light the fuse step back."

She didn't remember Peter doing that.

"Mr. Stanhope and Miss Noble, what on earth do you think you're doing?"

Sophie froze mid-flick. Caught in the act by Professor Critchton. What had made her think she could get away with such a feat? To make matters worse, Peter was draped over her in a most unbecoming fashion. Heat flooded her cheeks. She dropped the lighter and straightened abruptly, knocking her head into Peter's chin.

"Ow." Peter drew back, rubbing his jaw bone.

"Sorry." Sophie cringed. Peter just glared at her saying nothing. But facing Peter's irritation was better than Professor Critchton's anger. Peter could never stay mad at her for long, but the Professor was another matter. She peered at him trying to look contrite. Sure she was failing miserably.

"I'm very disappointed in the behavior of you two." He turned his attention to Peter. "How could you put Miss Noble in this kind of danger? Her skirt could have caught on fire, and that's the very least of it. Both of you could have lost fingers or worse."

"I understand your c-c-concern, Professor," Peter drew a finger along the length of his collar. "My f-f-father taught me to set off fireworks. Miss Noble was never in any danger."

"Is that right? You do know that in order to set fireworks off in a public place you need to have a license." Professor Critchton crossed his arms and looked down his nose at Peter. "As the university must clear this type of activity, I am sure you don't have one."

Peter's eyes grew wide. There were so many variables Sophie hadn't taken into account. This was supposed to be one final escapade not an academic infraction. Peter didn't say a word to defend himself. His face was red, and his lips trembled. Good Lord, he didn't have the stamina for this type of dressing down. Sophie had to do something to cut through the tension. "Professor, we didn't mean any harm. We were just having a bit of fun."

Professor Critchton turned on her. "Miss Noble, you two could have caused a lot of damage today. You should be grateful I intervened before something irreparable happened."

By now many of the attendees had gathered around them. To her dismay her father barreled toward them with long strides. Dear heaven, she was in for it now.

"Sophie, are you out of your mind?"

"Daddy, it was just a lark." The minute the words were out of her mouth she wished she could take them back. The thunderous look on her father's face was too much. She hadn't seen him in such a state since she'd snuck out of the house to go to a party when she was thirteen. This day was supposed to be a celebration, and all she had succeeded in doing was bring a load of retribution crashing down on her shoulders.

"We'll talk about this at home." Her father turned to the professor. "I duly apologize for my daughter's reckless behavior and will pay for whatever damage she has caused."

Professor Critchton surveyed the area. "It doesn't appear any lasting damage has been done. Miss Noble,

I expect to see you in my office tomorrow afternoon one o'clock sharp."

"Yes, sir." Sophie mumbled.

"Mr. Stanhope, I expect you to dispose of this nuisance safely. Understand I will be speaking with the Dean of your college in the morning."

Peter nodded still saying nothing.

Her father grabbed her arm. "Come on, Sophie, we're leaving."

Chapter Two

"What were you thinking?" Grandmama intoned in a dour impression of an empress. When exactly had she become the head of the Noble family? The one who meted out the punishment and the rewards. Sophie glanced at her mother whose eyes were glued to the floor. Her father wasn't much help either. His face had turned an unhealthy shade of purple, and his brown eyes burned with suppressed anger.

"I just wanted to have a little fun." Sophie held her chin high. She would not apologize for the fireworks anymore. This was supposed to be a celebration. "It was my day. It's not like I was standing inside a mausoleum. We were outside for goodness sake."

"Enough!" Grandmama slammed her cane onto the floor so hard the furniture shook. "What is wrong with you, child? Have you no thought for the reputation of your family?"

"It was a little harmless prank."

"Not so harmless, Sophie." Her head snapped in the direction of her father. She hadn't heard this kind of iciness in his voice for years. "You could have lit the grass on fire. Someone could have gotten hurt."

"Exactly so," her grandmama said with a nod.

Her mother raised her head. "Sophie, I am worried about your judgment. You don't know what you are doing."

"Peter did. He helps his father with the fireworks display in July. I would never have tried this if he hadn't had the experience I needed."

"You are missing the point," her father said. "You set fireworks off on college grounds. You are lucky no true damage was done. Still, they are considering discipline. You could be expelled."

"They wouldn't do that. I'm about to graduate."

"Not if they expel you. Your diploma isn't the certainty you think it is. Young ladies don't behave this way. Not to mention they have academic standards to uphold. They won't give a diploma to a behavioral problem."

"What? I'm not a behavioral problem," she screeched. "It was just a stupid prank."

"Sophie, you need to take this seriously." Her mother sat all prim and proper. This woman who never knew a day of joy or exuberance in her life was telling her to be serious. That was rich. How could she understand the need to have fun when she sucked the life out of anything enjoyable?

Follow the rules, Sophie. Behave yourself, Sophie. Never ever have an ounce of fun, Sophie. Then the axe fell.

"I think it's time you came to London," her grandmama said without ceremony. "I will teach you to be a lady."

"You can't do this," Sophie said with icy venom. "I still have time to find a job."

"No, child, you lost that opportunity with this last bit of foolishness. You can no longer be trusted." Her grandmama sniffed.

"Mother?" Sophie glanced at her mother who was studying her hands. She turned to her father. "Daddy?"

He glared back at Sophie grim-faced. "You have to the end of the week to get ready. We will not change our minds."

No one would come to her rescue. How had her life turned into this? "Please, Daddy, don't do this."

"I would do more than this if I could. If your Uncle Harry and Aunt Margaret hadn't made all the arrangements for your graduation party, I would forbid you from going. As it is, it is too late to make other arrangements. But make no mistake. You will be in London at the end of the week."

At the harshness of his words, Sophie turned tail and ran into her room. She flung herself on the bed. Her father agreed with her grandmama. Now she was sentenced to live in a drafty old house and attend stodgy old parties and talk to men twice her age. Even if she had to go, she would not get married. She sniffed. She still controlled her heart. She was in charge of that.

Feeling like the stupidest woman on earth, she pulled out her sketch pad and picked up her pencil. She scribbled the first thing that came to mind. Critchton. Why that stuffy old bore's face swam in her vision, she couldn't fathom. Her pencil flew across the page, carrying with it all the rage of the past few hours. Her parents' disappointment. Peter's pain. These were not the images a celebration should carry. When finished, she perused her work. As usual, she'd resorted to her favorite medium. The caricature. Critchton stood stiff-backed looking down his nose at an unworthy painting. Just like she'd seen him do at the MET.

She dropped her charcoal. In truth, the image was a bit harsh. It didn't capture his firm, broad shoulders or his soft brown eyes. Not that she should care about that. He was her nemesis. Still, her art should tell the truth. Too weary to rectify the matter, she pushed the pad away. Her head fell onto her pillow. She was the one who was inflexible. She was the immobile one. This wasn't what she wanted for herself. The fun-filled life as an artist she'd envisioned was drifting away so rapidly she was sure she'd be carried away by its force. Or by her grandmama's threat of imprisonment.

****

Sophie pulled dresses from the closet and threw them on the bed. Goodness, how had she amassed so many garments in the four years she had been at Roseline? Too many to fit into her small trunk. She sorted them into keep and give away piles. After she was finished, she looked at her work, but the piles became blurred by tears. She'd gotten herself into a pickle of a situation, and she didn't see any way out. She flopped down on the bed, tossing an arm over her eyes. What did it matter what clothing she kept? She was going to London away from all her friends and everything she knew.

A knock on the door drew her from her dark meanderings. With a sigh she pulled herself from the bed and opened the door.

"Hello, Sophie darling! Thought you might need some help packing." Maddie stood there all smiles. Her curly brown hair veritably bouncing with happiness. She sashayed into the room without an invitation. Not that Sophie wasn't happy to see her. There was just so much on her mind. Still it didn't pay to be rude.

"Would you like some tea?"

"No, I think I would prefer to get started." Maddie looked around the room. "This place looks like a hurricane tore through it."

"I'm trying to figure out what to keep and what to give away."

"Well," she said with her hands on her hips. "Let's get started then."

They worked in companionable silence for some time. Maddie would lift a garment. Sophie would tell her which pile it went into while Sophie sorted through her books. Each one of the books brought back too many memories. One on the great artists of the eighteenth century was the book that taught her about brush strokes and mixing paints for the exact right nuance. A book of poetry that she used for inspiration on themes. There must be fifty of them stacked up next to the wall. She couldn't keep all of them, but she didn't know which to leave behind.

Too overwhelmed to deal with it, she sat at the small table in her dorm room. "What am I going to do?"

"You're going to pack each item one at a time. Box them up and ship them out. Easy peasy."

"That's not what I meant." Sophie propped her chin on her fist. "This is supposed to be one of the happiest moments of my life. How'd it get so awful?"

Maddie walked over and sat across from her. "I doubt things are as bad as you suppose."

Sophie stood, waving her arms. "How can you say that? My parents can't stand me. That's bad enough. My grandmama wants to control my life, and the dean of my school wants to expel me."

"When you put it that way, I can see why you're in such a state."

"Exactly." Her point made she sat back down.

"However," Maddie leaned forward. "I hardly think your parents hate you. In fact, I know they love you and want what's best for you. Just as my parents want that for me, even when they make me feel insane."

"Then how can they send me to that drafty old mausoleum?" Sophie let her head drop into her hands. "My grandmama will make my life a living hell."

"That's true." Sophie's head shot up. Maddie put up a staying hand. "Before you bite my head off. It is well known that your grandmamma likes to rule the roost. We all know Aunt Charli had to runaway to get out from under her thumb."

"I know." Sophie rested her elbows on the table. A gesture her mother would have turned her nose downward on. *Sophie, ladies don't put their elbows on the table.* Always ladies do this or ladies do that. It was enough to make her head spin. From the way they were treating her, she was pretty sure she didn't qualify as a lady anymore. She wondered what that made her. Sophie hoped it made her unique. "That's what's so baffling. Why does she agree with grandmama?"

"Hmmm." Maddie had a far-off gaze. Her deep in thought look while she worked out a puzzle. In the years Sophie'd known her, she never thought that look would be used to sort out a catastrophe in her life. It struck her how her life had been virtually problem free until now. Curious. It wasn't like she hadn't gotten into trouble. Her parents had been mad at her more times than she could count. But everything had been fleeting. Nothing had stuck. But if she went to London, her carefree life would be over. If grandmama got her way, she'd be shackled by the end of a fortnight. "Aunt Jessie does say that your mother used to stand up for herself better."

"From all the stories she told me about her youth, you'd think she was a spitfire. But I can guarantee you that is not the case. Every time my grandmama is around, she cows to her will."

"What about your father?"

"Ugh, my father is very angry at me. He thinks I put the attendees at the garden party in danger."

"It was a very bold move." Maddie giggled.

"Too bold if you ask my father." Sophie leaned back. "No one in my family has a good sense of humor."

"Look." Maddie reached over and took Sophie's hand in hers. "Maybe you need to give your parents an opportunity to feel calmer. After a couple of days they might think differently about your grandmother's ultimatum."

"But what if they don't?"

"London isn't all that bad, you know." Maddie tilted her head. "I'll be there, and I'll introduce you to all my friends. We can go to all the museums and parks. It could be fun."

"If I'm even allowed out of the house without grandmama."

Maddie laughed. "It isn't the seventeenth century."

"Tell that to grandmama." Sophie crossed her arms over her chest.

Maddie smiled and went back to her puzzler gaze. "The biggest problem you seem to face is the school's response to your actions."

"Don't remind me." Sophie covered her face with her hand. "I have to go see Professor Critchton this afternoon."

"You mean that handsome fellow you apologized to yesterday?"

Sophie leveled Maddie with the most intimidating look she could muster. From the twinkle in her friend's eyes, she missed her mark. "Yes, but he's not that dishy."

"You've got to be joking. I saw you two making eyes at each other."

"I was not making eyes at him. He's the dean of the art department for goodness sake."

"You could have fooled me." Maddie leaned her chin on her hand. A mischievous smile lit her face. Good Lord, she thought this was funny. "I witnessed the sparks flying between you two."

"Sparks of anger and disdain." Sophie shot out of the chair. "Not ardor, I assure you."

"Calm down. I'm just teasing you."

"It's not funny." Sophie sunk back into her chair.

"All right, let's change the subject to something we both agree on." She reached into her purse and pulled out a newspaper clipping. She smoothed it out on the table. GRAYSON COLLECTION COMING TO ROSELINE MUSEUM. Sophie pulled the clipping for a closer view.

"The Grayson collection? I hear it's quite extensive." Her voice had lowered to the tone of reverence. "And it's coming to our little museum."

"I know." Maddie squealed. "I think we should go. It's the perfect thing to take your mind off your problems."

"Let's do it." Sophie looked around her small dorm room. Not much progress had been made since Maddie showed up. "But first we need to finish packing. Good thing the exhibit is a few days away. I hope that gives us enough time."

Maddie chuckled. How nice to have such supportive friends. Her spirits lifted. It was time to clean the clutter from her life. Time for a fresh new start.

****

Sophie entered the art department with less enthusiasm than usual. She didn't know what to expect, but from the butterflies churning in her stomach it wasn't going to be to her liking. Of course what could she expect? She was meeting with Professor Critchton, who would decide the fate of her status at the school. It was unfair that one small little prank had gotten blown out of proportion. Pun not intended.

She smoothed the skirt of her new walking dress knowing the black pinstripes accentuated her figure. This morning her instincts urged her to wear her new green dress complete with hat and gloves. It was always good to put one's best foot forward when trouble brewed in the distance. As an extra added bonus she brought along her portfolio just in case she had to seriously plead her case. Not that appearing respectable would increase her esteem in his eyes. Until her prank, there was nothing to distinguish her from the disdain he meted out to everyone. Lucky her, she had to go and get herself noticed.

She found the solid wood door with his nameplate and gave it a firm knock. No need to skirt about the subject. Best to deal with things head on. "It's open." A soft, feminine voice called from the other side. Sophie twisted the doorknob and entered into a waiting area.

A woman with graying hair that might have been a rich brown at one time sat behind a desk. She looked up and smiled at Sophie. "I'm sorry. I don't usually open the door after the lunch hour until 1:30. I had forgotten about Professor Critchton's appointment." She put one finger to her mouth in a "let's keep this our little secret" move. "Have a seat. I'll let him know you're here."

Sophie settled into the couch at the far end of the room. It wasn't an expansive waiting area. Just enough room for the secretary's desk, a coffee table, a couch, and two chairs. Still, there was a lot of wall space. Enough to display the artwork from past graduates as well as some prints of the works of more famous artists. It was strange seeing ornate frames against the sterile white walls of the college. They looked out of place. But that didn't deflect from the beauty of the still life and pastoral scenes. She was surprised the odious man who held her future in his hands was a better judge of art than she gave him credit for. The pieces were expertly selected and displayed to great advantage. Although many styles of art were exhibited from modern to renaissance, none of the selections clashed with the other.

The door at the other end opened, and the secretary emerged. "You can go in now, Miss Noble."

"Thank you." She made her way into Professor Critchton's office. It was filled with rich paneling with a bookshelf on one side that matched the cherry-wood color of the walls. A large wood desk occupied the center of the room which rested on top a plush oriental rug. Two chairs were placed in front of the desk. The man who was about to decide her future sat in an expensive leather chair.

He stood when she entered the room. "Welcome, Miss Noble. Please have a seat."

She did as he asked, clutching her portfolio in her lap. He sunk into his chair and glanced at her over steepled fingers for a few moments. He wasn't looking down on her exactly. However, there was an intensity in his gaze that indicated he was assessing her character. She sat stiff-backed waiting for him to speak. He had to speak first. If she did, she knew she'd end up groveling, and that just wouldn't do. She was determined to remain dignified.

"Miss Noble, I've met with our board regarding the events of graduation."

She nodded but said nothing. He didn't seem to notice her silence. He probably expected it. Fine upstanding people who followed the rules were what he wanted at the college. Not people who thought for themselves. Hopefully she looked the part because she sure didn't feel like the part.

"They are concerned with your disregard for the solemnity of our institution. Graduation from our college is a privilege not a right, Miss Noble. They have recommended expulsion."

A steel cord of dread wrapped around her insides, robbing her of breath. Expulsion. A wave of dizziness engulfed her as the room grew dim. She rubbed her forehead. Hoping for clarity in her moment of need. Logic came to her aid. "But I'm due to graduate in a week. How can they expel me?"

"You are a provisional graduate. Although you have completed your classwork, you won't officially be a graduate until your final grades are in. You fall into a limbo where they have every right to snatch your diploma from you."

"Expelled. My education means nothing. My grandmama spent all that money for nothing." She spoke to herself not realizing she'd said the words out loud. Her shame burned in her throat at the thought of her failure. Grandmama's claws dug in deeper, wrapping around her heart, signaling Sophie was about to embark on a life not her own.

"They haven't made their final decision." He leaned forward, his arms folded in front of him on the desktop. "Even if they expel you, you will be able to reapply for readmission in three years."

"Three years?" She gasped. "Over a stupid prank."

"Relax, Miss Noble, I don't think it will come to that. I've suggested a much simpler solution. It will allow you to have your diploma and hopefully solidify the lesson that your actions were rash and foolhardy."

"What do I have to do?" At this point, she would be willing to do almost anything. If it meant she would receive her diploma with no black mark on her record. That would mean she still had a chance to get a job before grandmama removed her from the country.

"Have you heard of the Grayson Collection?"

"Of course I have." She didn't mean to sound snippy, but did he think she was a ninny? Anyone who loved art as much as she did knew about the famous recluse who horded precious art.

"Well we're having an exhibition of his collection."

"I've heard." The course this conversation didn't seem that horrible. How bad could it be if they were discussing the Grayson collection? She might survive this ordeal after all.

"We need someone to collect tickets and check coats for us. I recommended you."

Her stomach plummeted to the floor. "What? You want me to check the coats?"

"Yes."

"But I won't get to see the exhibit."

"That's my offer, Miss Noble. If you think about it, I'm sure it's more preferable than expulsion."

She took a deep breath. Unfortunately, he was right. "Fine. I'll do it."

"Good." He smiled. He actually smiled. And it wasn't a malevolent one either. It was dazzling, exposing even white teeth and an adorable dimple in the center of his cheek. She sucked in a breath trying to get a handle on her conflicting emotions when she was around him. She didn't like him. She couldn't like him. He was everything she was not. Starchy. Judgmental. Proper. He followed the rules while she skirted around them. Which, the thought descended on her like a lead balloon, was why he sat in a plush office and she had gotten into trouble. "Be at the museum at 5:30 the evening of the exhibition. The gallery opens at 6:00, and the collection will be open for viewing at 7:00. Any questions?"

"No. I'll be there." She wasn't going to see the collection. She was going to be holed up in a cloak room collecting tickets and checking coats. How was she going to break the news to Maddie? "If you'll excuse me." She rose to leave. His voice stopped her.

"Hold on, Miss Noble, there's one more thing we need to discuss."

She sunk back into her chair. What now? "Yes?"

"I got a call from your Aunt Jessie the other night."

"I don't understand. Why would she call you?" It wasn't like Aunt Jessie to beg for mercy. She was a take your medicine and get over it type of gal. So what business could she have with Mr. Stiff Shirt?

"She tells me you would like to draw cartoons for a newspaper."

"I do. I just don't understand how that concerns you." She tried as best she could to erase the snippiness from her voice. His arched eyebrows let her know she'd failed. She clutched her portfolio tighter and waited to hear him out.

"She knew I had several connections with newspaper editors of prominent papers. Even with the fiasco at graduation, she hoped I might be of help to you."

"Why would someone who thought caricatures unworthy help me?" She was very bad at containing herself. If she continued in this vein, he might not be so willing to help her and more willing to destroy her career. Why didn't her tongue follow the very sage advice of her brain? Smile. Be ingratiating. If the man could be of service, why alienate him? Deep breaths. Calm down. "I'm sorry. I don't mean to be rude. You caught me off guard is all."

He grinned, not looking offended by her attitude. In fact he seemed to like it. He stood and walked around his massive desk to sit beside her. "Miss Noble, I think we got off on the wrong foot here. I thought by disposing of the unpleasant business first you would be more open to discussing your future as an artist. I see now it was not a good idea to broach both subjects in one sitting. If you'd like to take a day or two and come back, I would understand."

"No, we can talk now."

"I realized that I'm not familiar with your work. I see you brought your portfolio. Might I have a look?"

She handed it over uncertain of how the meeting had gone from bad to better. Life wasn't like that. She wasn't used to him being this close to her either. Usually, she was able to escape when he drew near. But this time she was in his office. He'd offered to do her a favor. She couldn't leave.

He opened her portfolio. She wasn't sure she liked the idea of his scrutinizing her work. So she focused on his profile. Maddie was right. He was quite attractive. He had a strong chiseled chin, and his nose wasn't nearly as long as she had supposed. His lips were full and...

Crap! His nose. The caricature she drew the other night was in her portfolio. How stupid of her. Why hadn't she removed the blasted thing? She needed to get her portfolio back before he saw it. But she couldn't think of a way to do that gracefully.

"If you'd like, I could pull out my best pieces for you."

He looked up. "I'd like to get a picture of all your work. Many things can be discerned from all your works, not just the best ones."

He flipped the page. Oh could he please stop before he got to the last one? She'd grabbed her sketch book on habit. It went everywhere with her. After all, inspiration struck in the most unusual surroundings. It was her bad luck inspiration had struck after the horrid events of the garden party. She should have destroyed the picture the minute she had created it.

"You have a very fine technique, Miss Noble."

"Thank you." She stopped herself from uttering "are you done?"

"You have a very good grasp of the ironic in your political sketches."

"Thank you." Oh please have seen enough. But with every flip of the page he got closer to the dreaded drawing. She could see no good way of getting out of this one. Just when the man had offered help, she was going to lay the biggest insult on him. These days she could do nothing right. She sat in silence waiting for the other shoe to drop.

It hit the ground with a huge grunt. He looked at his likeness. A skinny arched back. An overly defined rear end. That stupid long nose. He must think she was the embarrassment the board thought her.

He glanced in her direction. Oddly enough no anger burned in the depth of his brown eyes. There was an emotion she couldn't name. Disappointment? Pain? She wasn't sure. But she was certain he wasn't insulted. Something else flickered beneath the surface. Even though she didn't know what it meant, she felt worse than if she had angered him.

"Not a very good likeness is it?"

"I can explain."

"No need, Miss Noble." He handed the sketchbook back to her without ceremony. Then he positioned himself behind his desk. Separated from her. Back to the business side of things. Why should that leave her cold inside? "I've seen enough. I expect you to be on time the day of the exhibition."

"I won't be late." She got up and shot out of the office fighting back tears. Dread burned in her breast. She didn't know what had happened, but it was more than losing a job opportunity. And that thought upset her. She could find a job on her own, but she was walking away from a different sort of opportunity. One she had no name for.

Chapter Three

"May I see your ticket?" Sophie stood behind a well-worn counter in the mustiest cloak room ever. She hadn't seen Professor Critchton since their meeting. It wasn't like she saw him every day, but she was sure he would greet her at the museum. The fact he did not spoke volumes. She was wrong. She had insulted him. He was angry at her. Maybe it was better he wasn't around.

The man on the other side of the counter handed her his two tickets. She marked them. "Would you like to check your hat or something?" She was really bad at this. This lesson was going to last a long time. It was absolute torture, but she smiled brightly as the man across from her handed her his hat. She gave him a claim ticket.

"Thank you, Miss." He grabbed the ticket and headed off into the gallery. Sophie leaned forward as far as the stall would allow and watched as the man entered gallery. She couldn't see anything but the hallowed portal into a world she would miss because she had to man her station. She couldn't even catch a glimpse of one painting. A barring wall created a hallway for the crowd to turn left or right. But for her it was a tragic barrier. Why couldn't they have put at least one painting on that wall? No matter how far she craned her neck none of the precious collection came into view. At least Maddie was inside and would be able to describe it to her in good detail. That would have to be enough, she supposed.

"Goodness, child. What are you doing draping from that counter like a ragamuffin?" Her grandmama's strident admonishment clued her in that she was once again a disappointment to her family legacy. She slipped off the counter. Feet firmly on the ground, she gave her grandmama her most ingratiating smile. Of course her family was here. Half of Boston was here. But did they have to witness her humiliation?

"Good evening, Grandmama, may I see your ticket please?" She was not about to explain herself. Being cloistered inside this box of a room was enough punishment. It didn't help that her whole family was going to see the collection of the century knowing she was unable to go. Grandmama handed over her ticket, her disapproval with Sophie's disgrace never fading from her expression. She ripped it apart and handed her half of it. "Is there anything you'd like to check?"

Grandmama shook her head. Sophie's mother took her place in line. "Are you doing all right, Sophie?"

She nodded, tearing her ticket in half with less force than Grandmama's. The concern floating in the depths of her mother's green eyes kept her from speaking her mind. Her mother really was concerned about her. Maybe her concern would be enough to keep Sophie in the States. She could work that angle. Surely, she didn't want Sophie to suffer the same fate as Grandmama had wanted for her. She'd told her more than once she was fated to marry an ogre. Not only didn't she know him, but he was cruel. If this was the type of man Grandmama approved of, how could she send Sophie to London? There had to be a way to get through to her.

"You can walk through hell if you know you're going to get out, darling." Daddy flashed her the "you'll always be daddy's girl" smile. This time, it didn't warm her heart and make her feel special like it had when she was a teenager. No, this time a slow simmer of frustration rose to the top of her frayed nerves. He wanted to act like nothing huge had happened. Like he hadn't threatened to send her away. Honestly, it was a bit too much. But she wasn't about to let him know this.

"So you've always said." Sophie looked past him to see if her brother was also here to snicker at her. He wasn't. "Where's Nathan?"

"We left him at the hotel," Daddy said. "He had some reading he wanted to catch up on before the summer starts."

"Of course he did." The golden boy was at it again. Currying the favor of their parents. The perfect child. But if he didn't get out more, he was going to be a pale, thin wraith. However was he going to survive college? But that was not her problem.

"Well," her mother said a little too brightly. "We'll see you after the show."

"Okay." She tried not to sound glum. Her eyes followed them until they were around the hated barrier. This time she made sure to keep her feet on the floor and her back straight. She didn't need any more admonishments tonight. The trickle of participants turned into a steady stream, keeping her busy for the next forty-five minutes. After the last one passed into the gallery, she was left alone to think about what she'd done.

For the life of her, she couldn't fathom why everyone was making a huge deal about her antics. Her family had known her all her life. They knew she pulled pranks. The school, on the other hand, didn't necessarily know her proclivity for fun. Most of the pranks she pulled were on her friends. Off campus and away from prying eyes. Now that she thought about it, she couldn't figure out what made her think she could get away with such a huge feat.

Peter and Sophie had been so excited about the prospect of fireworks. It would be the biggest, best prank she had pulled ever. In the end they'd just egged each other on. It seemed so harmless. Peter knew what he was doing after all. What better way to showcase her achievements than through a display of art with the sky as the backdrop? But it had all gone so wrong. Sophie pushed a pen back and forth on the counter contemplating every way to dig herself out of this hole.

"Sophie, what are you doing parked behind a counter?"

Sophie looked up into the earnest face of her friend Peter. His glittering blue eyes held the earnest gleam of a graduate ready to be off on his next adventure. His slight build had not quite caught up to his future life as a businessman. Wiry and slim, his shoulders didn't quite fill out his tuxedo. "Doing my penance it would seem. You look well."

He gripped the counter like he was about to topple over any second. What was up with him? "I've been wanting to talk to you since the garden party. I didn't mean to get you in trouble."

Sophie sighed. "You didn't. This is all my fault. Not everyone was amused by our little prank."

"Well I thought the idea was brilliant. The fireworks were marvelous."

"They were, weren't they?" Sophie giggled in spite of her situation. She would never forget how the colors lit the sky. Then reality crashed down on her. "My parents want to send me to London to teach me a lesson."

"Wait." His face screwed up, looking like he'd just bit into a lemon. "Why?"

"Apparently I am a behavior problem."

His eyes grew wide. "I could take the blame and tell them I roped you into it. It's not like I would face any consequences. My father would take care of that."

That was her Peter. Always ready to charge in like a white knight and save the day. If only he looked the part. "That's very kind of you, but I can take care of myself."

"Look." He took her hand in his. Sophie was sure he was trying to comfort her, but his light touch did nothing to ease her mind. "Would it help if my father talked to the school? I'm confident he could clear this matter up. And then you can stay here."

His gaze was so hopeful she almost laughed. "You don't know my parents. They have no sense of humor. They've made their mind up to send their disgrace of a daughter away."

He huffed, letting go of her hand. "What does sending you to England accomplish?"

"They think they are going to marry me off to some stuffy lord or some sort."

A slow smile spread across his face. He slapped his open hand on the counter so hard it shook. "Oh, I get it. I think I might have a solution for that. Hang on."

He sped away and slipped around the barring wall. His actions so incongruous with the conversation it bordered on abrupt. A solution. There wasn't any solution except for her to find employment here in the States. Then they couldn't send her away.

Peter came back carrying two glasses of champagne. The spring in his step was like he held the crown jewels. What had gotten into him? He handed her a glass, his eyes darting looking left and right, then lit on Sophie.

"I'm not sure you can bring drinks out here," Sophie whispered.

"It's fine." He waved off the suggestion. "I guarantee we won't get in trouble this time. Look, do you mind if I join you?"

"What are you about?" Sophie unlatched the door, and Peter walked through.

"Look, I leave after graduation to take my place in my father's business." He paused considering his words carefully. "We've known each other for a long time and have jolly good fun. There isn't a moment in my college career that doesn't have you in it."

"I've had a great time too. You're one of my closest friends." A shimmer of dread crept up her spine.

"Well, yes," He drew a finger around his collar. He inched closer. "But it's more than that."

Sophie's hand gripped the glass flute so hard she feared it might break. "I don't understand."

"Right." His face turned a deep crimson. "You know I set those fireworks for you."

"Yes, we planned the event together."

"Exactly." His face softened into relief. It was like he was certain she caught his meaning, but she had no idea where this was going. He extricated the glass from her grasp and took her hand in his. Covering it with his other hand. "The thing is, I'd do anything for you. Anything you ask, it's yours. I swear."

His gaze couldn't meet hers. After all years she'd known him, she'd never seen him this nervous or at a loss for words. Nothing he was saying made any sense. "That's very sweet."

"So I've been thinking. We get along so well that maybe you might consider coming back to Michigan with me."

"I don't want to go to Michigan. I want to get a job here in Boston."

He swallowed. "I'm sorry, I'm botching this up."

"What are you talking about?"

"I love you, Sophie. From the first moment I met you, I knew you and I were meant to be together. Would you do me the honor of being my wife?"

"Oh, Peter." His declaration, although sweet, wasn't what she expected. They had never been on anything but group dates. She'd never considered his feelings ran deeper than two chums having fun. With the exception of a few chaste wet kisses, there'd been nothing to indicate he had any affection deeper than friendship. "I'm sorry, but I can't return your affections. I thought we were just friends."

"How could you think that?" he sputtered, letting her hand go. "After all we've done together."

"We were never alone. I had no idea you felt this way."

"You prefer London to me?"

"It's not that simple." Sophie wracked her brains for the right thing to say. The tortured look on his face burned into her soul. Their time together had been such fun. He was a dear friend. She didn't want to hurt his feelings any more than necessary. This just wasn't fair. She was pretty sure she hadn't led him on, but what other explanation could there be for the circumstance they found themselves in now? "If I led you to believe there was something more than friendship, I'm sorry. I thought we were just having fun. You are very dear to me. But I can't marry you. I don't love you."

His eyes glazed over into a hard, cruel surface. She'd never seen him this angry. Come to think of it, she'd never seen him angry. He'd always been happy and docile. The perfect chum to pull pranks with. "I can't believe it. All this time I've wasted on a silly girl who can't take things seriously. I misjudged you."

"I think it's best you leave." Sophie pointed toward the exit. Peter was probably just lashing out in anger, but his words still stung.

"Wait, I didn't mean that. I'm sure you can come to love me in time." He grabbed her and pulled her to him. He pressed his lips against her forcing her backward. The counter's edge jammed into her back caging her. She pushed him a way.

"Peter, stop." She wiped her lips.

"Not until I show you we're meant to be together."

"Am I interrupting something?" The rich baritone she was beginning to recognize elicited both irritation and joy. How was it Professor Critchton always caught her in the most compromising position?

"No," Peter said. "The lady and I were just having a discussion."

Professor Critchton looked down his nose at Peter. Never had she been so happy to see that expression. "It doesn't look like a discussion to me."

"You need to mind your own business, sir." Peter sputtered. The words were brash, but he didn't look so comfortable now.

"What goes on at this college is my business." Professor Critchton commanded the room even from the other side of the counter. It was enough to stop Peter from pawing her. Sophie stood a little straighter smoothing out her skirt and replacing the pins that had fallen from her hair. She stopped mid-sweep all of a sudden, aware of how vain those actions were. She hastily replaced the last pin and let her hands drop to her side.

"This is a private matter." Peter said.

"Not when it occurs on school property and you are caught accosting one of its students." Professor Critchton leaned in, a foreboding gleam in his eyes.

"I w-w-would never." Peter's face turned ashen. He yanked open the door. His words trailed down the hallway. "My father will hear about this insult."

"Thank you." She smiled weakly at Professor Critchton. So grateful he showed up when he did. She had misjudged someone she had known for years. That was disappointing enough. Now it appeared she been wrong about Professor Critchton too. She gave him her full attention. He filled out his tux in a way that Maddie would call delicious. If she was being honest, she had to admit he looked appealing. He was the most pleasant face she'd seen tonight.

"Are you al lright?" His face softened with concern. It was enough to make her burst into tears. And she wasn't going to let that happen.

"Yes." She sniffed. "I just don't understand how I could have been so wrong about Peter."

He gazed down the hall. "Character always reveals itself during stress."

"So it would seem."

He leaned in close enough for her to smell his aftershave. Spearmint and sage if she didn't miss her guess. Such a pleasant scent she breathed deeply savoring the calmness that washed over her. Sophie clamped down on a giggle. Resolved not to appear girlish in front of him. She wanted him to take her seriously. To see her as a woman who was capable of holding down a job at a newspaper or periodical. Special enough to be considered a real artist.

Her serenity cascaded into guilt at the thought of how mean she'd been in drawing that stupid picture. He was being so kind it caught her off guard. Sometimes, maybe close to all the time, she had no filter. No ability to think things through. "Sorry about the caricature."

His serious eyes considered her, but for the first time his gaze didn't feel judgmental. His expression was much kinder than she expected at the mention of the doodle drawn by a silly, impetuous girl. "We all do things we regret when we're angry."

"I suppose." Sophie looked down, unable to meet his eyes. He was much nicer than she'd originally thought. Less rigid than her imagination painted him. She prided herself on being such a good judge of character. Yet she'd gotten him wrong.

A woman with gray hair and equally drab clothing approached. Sophie took a step back and readied to take the ticket of this latecomer. Professor Critchton smiled and waved. "Hello, Agnes."

"Hello, sir." As the woman drew closer, she recognized her as the Professor's secretary.

"I think you've been tortured enough," Professor Crichton said. "Agnes has agreed to take the rest of your shift so you can enjoy the exhibit."

"Really?" Sophie almost stood on her tiptoes and kissed his cheek. Almost. Instead she twirled around not caring how silly she looked. She was going to see the Grayson collection! Then a thought stopped her short. She put her hands to her cheek. "Oh no, I forgot I gave my ticket to Iris."

"You don't need a ticket." He stood stiff-backed, but he didn't look stuffy. He looked proud. "You shall go as my guest."

"Thank you." Sophie ran around the counter into the hallway before he could change his mind. He offered his arm. She took it wondering how she could ever have considered him odious. They walked into the gallery with walls lined with so many paintings she couldn't figure out where to look first.

"Why don't you take a look around?" Professor Critchton directed her to the right side and then took off for a group of his cronies in the center of the floor. Professor Overton was among them. She caught his eye and waved. Maybe he had something to do with Professor Critchton's change of heart. He smiled and nodded. Then she headed off to look at the collection.

Maddie found her examining a very fine oil painting done by Renoir. She took her hands and squealed. "I'm glad you were able to make it. Isn't this fabulous."

"What I've seen so far is superb." She looked around the room for a familiar brunette. "Where's Iris?"

"She's over there speaking with a few wealthy gents."

Sophie glanced in the direction Maddie indicated. There Iris was laughing and talking. One of the gents offered her a glass of champagne. She took it with zeal. "Hope springs eternal for that one."

"Too true. But at least I now have someone who appreciates artwork as much as I do."

"Indeed you do." Sophie took her arm and strolled along with her taking in the various works of art. "It's a shame this is a private collection. This art should be open to the public every day."

"I can't disagree." Maddie said. "But at least we get to see it now. And they have a newly discovered Degas. A Degas. Can you believe it?"

"This I've got to see. Do you think it's the one you're looking for?"

"I don't know yet. But I have never seen this one before." Maddie's excitement was contagious. If this was Maddie's Degas, it was quite a find. "It's right this way."

Maddie led her through the meandering guests until they reached a group of twenty or so people crowded around a painting. They pulled closer. Sophie heard very audible gasps of appreciation and other exclamations.

"Where did Grayson get such a find?" an elderly woman said.

"Do you think it was stolen by the Nazis?" the gentleman beside her said.

"Well how did it get to Grayson?" a man on the other side of the crowd murmured.

"Who cares? It is quite beautiful, don't you think," a very expensively dressed woman said. Anxious to see the painting that had captured so much attention, Sophie pushed through the crowd ignoring the grunts of disapproval. One woman muttered "well I never" as she passed. Sophie ignored them all. It was too important to see this rare find.

What Sophie saw stopped her short. It couldn't be. This time she should be mistaken. Grayson was known to be very careful about the art he collected. Down to the most minute detail in the provenance. He had it all investigated by his art experts. So how did this painting get into his collection? She pressed closer looking for any detail to prove her wrong.

This was not Maddie's Degas, it was hers. She remembered painting the very curve in the ballerina's arm as she extended for an arabesque. Each ballerina behind her bent in a plie or stretching on the bar. The curve of the ballet slipper as she pointed her outstretched toe. She'd had such trouble with the shading of the slipper, but it had come out well in the end. Still, it was surprising the experts hadn't noticed that little detail. Maybe they'd passed it off as one of his early works. She guessed that was possible.

Sophie glanced at the signature. Underneath the Degas was the Celtic symbol she'd put on each one of her class projects. It stood out so much for her she was aghast the experts didn't notice the irregularity. Her Van Gough hung in the MET. Her Degas here amidst

Grayson's collection. The room dimmed. She was so lightheaded she took a step back. She thought Professor Overton was going to take care of this. Surely, he'd recognized this painting. Maybe he hadn't viewed the whole collection yet. She had to warn him.

A hand grasped her elbow. "Are you all right?" Maddie asked. "You look so pale."

"I can't believe this is happening."

"What are you talking about?" Maddie led her out of the crowd to an empty area. Sophie breathed in fresh air. Her vision cleared. She felt steadier.

"That's my painting hanging over there."

"The Degas?" Maddie gasped. "You must be imagining things. Grayson isn't the type to buy a painting without the approval of an expert."

"I know that, but it's mine." Sophie grabbed her arm. "Do you remember me telling you that I put the Celtic symbol meaning four friends at the bottom of all my signatures?"

"Vaguely." She had on her puzzle face again.

"Well check it out. It's there."

"All right." Maddie made her way into the crowd again. Sophie waited the ten minutes for her to extricate herself. She walked toward her as pale as Sophie must have looked moments before. "You're right. It's there. How is that possible?"

"That's what I intend to find out." Sophie headed in Professor Overton's direction. Maddie pulled her back.

"I wouldn't do that. You have no idea what's going on. You've been in enough trouble lately."

"But this is wrong. He promised me he would look into this. I just don't understand how he could have overlooked this other painting missing from the catacombs. I mean look at him chortling over there with his cronies."

"Maybe he didn't look that closely. He can't remember every painting a student does in his classroom."

"Maybe." She looked in his direction. The ease of his manner and discourse indicated he was unaware of the forgery. But that didn't seem possible when there was such a buzz about the newly found Degas. He would have taken a look. She found it hard to believe he'd be so cavalier in his examination of such a find. Sophie didn't like the conclusion her train of thought had taken her. It was best to give him the benefit of the doubt. "Then I should let him know."

"Sophie, think about what you're doing," Maddie said.

"I am." Sophie waltzed over to the group of men. Professor Critchton smiled at her approach. In stark contrast, Professor Overton ignored her. He was looking inkier by the minute. But she would not be thwarted. She tapped his shoulder. He looked at her. "Can I have a word with you?"

"Miss Noble, haven't you been told it is rude to interrupt a conversation?"

"I wouldn't normally," she muttered. "But this is important."

"Very well," he said wearily. "What's this about?"

"Remember the matter we discussed a few days ago?"

"Of course." His eyes narrowed.

"Well it's happened again."

"Miss Noble, I hardly think that is the case. You are talented but not that talented."

Sophie looked around at the rest of the men viewing the scene with interest. She didn't want to embarrass her mentor, so she pulled him further away. "You don't understand. It's the Degas. That's my painting," she said under her breath.

"You're imagining things. There's no way Grayson's experts would allow a forgery into his collection."

"I am not imagining things." Her voice rose attracting more onlookers. She lowered her voice. "It's mine. I swear."

"You think too highly of yourself, Miss Noble." His voice rose above the crowd.

"But you said you would look into this," Sophie screeched, not caring how many onlookers they had. This was too important. She couldn't have her paintings passed off as the real thing. If she allowed such a thing, she would be guilty of a crime. "I thought you took this seriously. The Degas was painted by me, and you know it."

She hadn't meant to say the last part. It just slipped out in her anger at his treatment of this issue. From the way his jaw dropped he hadn't expected her to do that either. He recovered fairly quickly. He yanked his arm from her grasp. "Seriously? With all the pranks you pull no one takes you seriously, Miss Noble. If you will excuse me."

With a poorly executed bow, he left. Sophie stood in the center of the floor. All eyes on her as the burn of humiliation crept up her neck and filled her cheeks. This day couldn't get any worse if she had awoken this morning with the intention of having a bad day. What was clear, her mentor who had been so attentive and encouraging in the beginning, was somehow involved with this debacle. If she were to rectify this calamity, she would have to take matters into her own hands.

"My child," Grandmama's grating voice chimed in behind me. "Is there no boundary to your insolence?"

Sophie whirled on her, too far gone to even consider the implications of what she was about to say. "I'm not lying. All you want to do is dictate to me. But you haven't ever considered that I might be in the right."

"That's enough, Sophie." Her mother interceded. "I think we should take our leave now."

"Fine."

"Don't be so disrespectful to your mother." Her father guided her toward the exit. Sophie noted he'd left out her Grandmama from the chastisement. She hoped that was on purpose.

****

Raymond Critchton watched as Miss Noble's family escorted her out of the gallery. Miss Noble was truly a little spitfire right down to her pert little nose and passionate brown eyes. She was very amusing. The only thing that bothered him was how she saw him. If the caricature was any indication, she thought him stuffy and overbearing. He supposed it wasn't unusual for a student to view the dean of the department that way. He just didn't want her to see him that way.

Then there was this business with Professor Overton. From what he discerned, Miss Noble claimed she painted the Degas. What an odd thing to claim. Odder still was the defensive way Overton rebuffed her.

Almost as if he were hiding something. Perhaps he was being unkind to poor Overton. Raymond was well aware Overton had applied for his job. That he was a bit put off Raymond had been offered the position. They managed to keep things as civil as possible. However, if Overton could find a way to oust him from his job, he'd do it without another thought.

It was important not to give Overton the opportunity. That meant not questioning him until he had more proof to go on. There were rumors that forgeries connected with Roseline's college had surfaced. Since the reputation of the college was on the line, it was up to him to investigate the matter. After all, that's why he'd been hired. There were more people than Overton who could be involved. Including the cronies he'd stood with a minute ago.

Raymond headed toward the painting that had caused so much controversy in the short time it had hung in the gallery. He moved in-between the onlookers to get a full view of the ballerina. The style was Degas. The choice of colors was Degas. The subject matter was typical of Degas. If he could get closer. Examine the makeup of the paint. View the provenance. He might have a clearer understanding of what was going on.

His eyes lit on the signature in the corner. It was a spot on match of Degas'. But on closer inspection there was something amiss. Underneath the signature was a tiny symbol. He had no idea of the meaning behind it, but he'd seen it before. He just couldn't place where. Then it hit him. That symbol was under the signature of the Van Gough that hung in the MET.

Ah yes, things were beginning to make sense. He'd seen that same symbol on three paintings hanging at Club 501. The paleness of Miss Noble's skin that day at the MET when they spoke about the Van Gogh. He slapped his hand against his forehead. How had it taken so long for things to add up?

"Couldn't resist another peek, eh, Critchton?" Overton shouldered his way between Raymond and the man standing next to him.

"Certainly a curiosity, wouldn't you say?"

"I don't quite catch your meaning, sir."

"Don't you think it odd that one of your students claims to have painted this Degas?"

He shook his head as if embarrassed by the spectacle. "You can't take Miss Noble seriously. She's a very misguided girl."

"Be that as it may." Raymond couldn't quite disagree with Overton's assessment, but he wanted to smack the man all the same. "Isn't it your practice to have your students imitate the greats to get a feel for their technique?"

"Absolutely." Overton paused as if considering his words carefully. Raymond looked down the very nose Miss Noble had poked fun at. He wondered how often he did that. "But the students don't create their own works. They copy directly from works already created by the great ones."

"I see." Critchton looked back at the object of their discussion. He wondered if Overton had missed the small symbol in the lower right-hand corner. The experts obviously had or had dismissed it as an anomaly of this one painting. If different experts had authenticated the Van Gough and the Degas, they wouldn't put two and two together as Raymond had. He had no doubt Miss Noble had painted this picture.

"If you'd like to get a feel for my curriculum, I could take you down to the catacombs and show you some work the students left behind."

"I just might do that." For one thing, he needed to find out what the man was hiding.

Chapter Four

Back in the hotel suite, Sophie stood next to the dining room table far away from the glittering stares of her mother, father, and grandmama. Her knees were so weak she thought she might have to grab hold of the edge to keep standing. The cushioned chairs around the table were inviting, but she refused to sit. She would not take the weaker position. This time they needed to listen to her.

"What has gotten into you, child? You are behaving like a hooligan." Grandmama glared at her with a baleful look while she sat stiffly on the sofa chin raised. She was so sure Sophie was a misbehaving child. She would not be chastised any longer.

"It wasn't a prank," Though her fingers trembled, her voice remained calm. She didn't know how she avoided shrieking. "I painted that Degas. You have to believe me."

"I can't believe you are confessing to forging a painting. Do you know how much trouble you are in?" Her father's expression was stern but not without compassion.

"It was an assignment, Daddy." She hated the whine in her voice. Why did she have to plead with him to know she was telling the truth? She had never lied to him in her life. Well, at least not about anything significant. And this was important. "It wasn't meant to be seen by anyone other than Professor Overton."

"Why on earth would your Professor ask you to forge a painting?" Grandmama leaned on her cane, her steel gray eyes shining with a malevolent glimmer. Sophie shuddered. To think that Mama had been raised under this tyrant was unthinkable. She turned to her mother, but her eyes were glued to the floor as usual, twisting her hands together. Where had the woman with the guts to stand up to her grandmama gone? As it was, Sophie could expect no help from her.

"He didn't ask me to forge a painting. My class was learning new techniques, and our assignment was to paint in the style of Degas, Renoir, Van Gough, and other famous artists. Professor Overton thought if we learned how the greatest artists worked our own style would emerge."

"And did it?" Grandmama's lips pursed in disapproval.

"I'm actually more of a cartoonist. Painting isn't really my thing."

"Then how is it you claim to be able to fool the experts?" Grandmama raised her eyebrows. "Seems a bit far-fetched if you ask me."

Sophie didn't think this was any of her grandmama's business, but that hadn't ever stopped her from butting her holier than thou nose into her family's business. Sophie rubbed her hands together and paced the floor hoping her father would say something, but he was remaining uncharacteristically silent. His mouth drooped in disappointment and he appeared to be looking inward. He was working on a solution. In most cases, the outcome was a good one. In this case, Sophie wasn't hopeful.

"The thing is, Professor Overton liked my paintings. He encouraged me to do more in the hopes I would be more comfortable with oil painting. But it is a tedious process, and I got no real joy out of it. Still he was impressed with what I had produced."

"And how did it happen that this painting fell into the Grayson collection?" Grandmama asked.

"That's what I can't figure out. I never removed them from the school. When I discovered the painting at the MET, I went directly to Professor Overton. That's why I was so mad that the Degas surfaced."

"There's another one?" Grandmama was aghast. "When was that?"

"A few days ago."

"Why didn't you come to me immediately?" her father asked.

"You weren't here yet." He was the first one she should have gone to. That was very clear now. But Sophie couldn't bear to have him look at her with disapproval the way he did now. She'd always been the apple of his eye. Mama accused him of being wrapped around Sophie's fingers. She'd always liked that. But something like this. His daughter a criminal. So unbelievable yet true. Even if unintentional was more than he could take. "I thought my professor would take care of it. But now it appears he may be involved."

"Are you suggesting that a highly respected professor is involved in selling forgeries?" Grandmama asked.

"What other explanation could there be? He all but tried to discredit me tonight. What reason would he have to do that if he wasn't involved?"

That shut her up. Sophie was never so happy to hear silence. Criticism wasn't going to help. What she needed was a plan. A way to expose the people who'd put her in the middle of this debacle.

"Exactly how many did you paint?" Her father had finally found his voice.

"No more than ten."

"Where are the others?"

"They're stored in the catacombs at the school."

"We need to collect them immediately."

"Are you out of your mind?" Grandmama asked. "There is no need to sully our name more than it already has been. I've booked passage for Sophie and myself after graduation. Once she is safely in England, this dreadful business should be over. What's important is she keep her mouth shut so she will not implicate herself any further. No one is taking her seriously at this point. No need to press the matter."

"I need to clear my name."

"There is nothing to clear, child. No one believes you. No one is investigating the matter."

Well that wasn't exactly true. She was investigating and she wouldn't stop until she got to the bottom of what was going on. Her paintings would not be used to bleed money off of unsuspecting folks. It wasn't right. She wasn't raised to allow people to be taken advantage of.

****

The next morning Raymond headed to the gallery to get a closer look at the painting. He met the gallery official at the door. With a turn of a key, they were inside. It would be good to finally get this business dealt with. After his meeting with Overton yesterday he was sure the man was involved in the forgery ring. More surprising was Miss Noble's involvement. Given she was telling everyone with the finesse of a town crier, it was evident she was an innocent in the matter.

Still, it took several people to pawn off forgeries successfully. Overton was not acting alone. Miss Noble had painted the items in his art class. But who else was involved?

"I removed the Degas as requested, sir," the official said. "It is waiting for us in the back room."

"Thank you, Tony. I appreciate your help in this matter."

"My pleasure. Miss Noble is a very nice lady. Anything I can do to clear this mess up, I will do."

"Good to know."

Tony led him to the back room where four large tables occupied most of the rooms. One held a golden statue of an eagle. Another a glass case with a ceramic bowl painted in Native American designs. The last table held the Degas. Ray peered closely at the artwork. It really was an excellent reproduction. The brush strokes, coloring, and style a complete replica of Degas. The only blemish in the whole piece was the odd little symbol in the lower right corner.

It still perplexed him how the expert had missed it. He supposed it could be overlooked as a paint splatter. Or even something intended to be there. If he hadn't seen it on the other painting, he might have dismissed the irregularity too. As long as everything else lined up. It was hard to believe that was the case.

"Who authenticated this piece?"

"Master Archer, sir."

"I don't recall him being one of Grayson's usual experts."

"He isn't. He was employed by the gallery that sold the painting to Grayson."

Raymond pulled the painting up to view the back of the canvas. There were very few stamps on the back. It didn't appear the painting had traveled through museums. Instead, the painting had been through five galleries. The most recent being the Infinity Gallery. "Do you have the provenance handy?"

"Absolutely." Tony walked over to a locked cabinet. He pulled a key ring from his belt and opened it. He rifled through several folders before he pulled one out. He laid it on the table next to the painting. Ray yanked it toward him and rifled through it. According to the provenance, the painting had been through five owners. All had been private collectors. However, it was odd that no one knew about this painting before now.

"Why are we just hearing about this painting now?"

"The way I heard it, this painting has been in the Darton family attic for over forty years. It was considered lost. When it got discovered, the Darton family donated it to the gallery for charitable purposes who sold it to Grayson."

"Why didn't Grayson use his usual expert?"

"He was unavailable. Master Archer comes highly recommended."

Then why had he never heard of him? This situation was getting stranger and stranger by the minute. Was Grayson so desperate to own a Degas that he didn't go through his usual meticulous inquiry? Sure the Infinity Gallery had a very good standing in the artist community and did not have the reputation for passing off fakes. But stranger things had been known to happen. "This whole thing doesn't make any sense."

"Professor Critchton, I like Miss. Noble. But isn't it possible that this is just a prank of hers? You can see by the provenance everything is in order. The certificates are all accounted for. They have been authenticated. The experts say this is a genuine Degas."

"I know." But Ray wasn't about to let this go. "Did anyone say anything about the symbol in the corner there?"

"Not that I can see."

It was time to visit the catacombs and see the works of these students. Something was very wrong here. Overton most certainly was behind it. The only question was who else was involved.

****

Sophie stepped down the cracked cement stairs making sure her skirt didn't catch on anything. Her father followed behind her. She hated the musty dark place that the students were forced to store their paintings in. She brushed a cobweb away stifling a shudder as she made her way to her locker. She swung the door open and blinked.

Empty. The only thing that was there was the bare wood floor, bits of paper, and an errant pastel. Father strode up behind her peering over her shoulder. Sophie gasped. "I don't understand. They're gone."

"This doesn't look like a great place to store art," her father said. "Is it possible they could have been removed to another location?"

"I don't think anyone would do that without telling me," she said trailing her finger along the door frame. She walked down the aisle peering into other stalls. Everything was gone. The stalls held nothing. Where had all the art gone?

A spindly shiver of terror shot down her spine. Sophie's head spun. This couldn't be happening. How had eight of her paintings disappeared overnight? Professor Overton was responsible, she was sure of it. Now how could she prove she'd created the paintings?

The guard approached them. Stooped over, steadying himself with one hand on the stalls. "Who's there?"

"It's me, Mr. Mortimer."

"Miss Noble, what on earth are you doing here?"

"I wanted to show my father my paintings, but they're gone."

"Didn't you get the notice?"

"What notice?"

Mortimer put his hands in his pockets and looked at her with the concern of a doting grandfather. He'd been with the school for forty years caring for the students' property. He'd always been kind to her. Always looked after her welfare. His eyes traveled to the ceiling as if what he had to tell her was posted there. "The notification went out about a week ago that the students needed to clean out their lockers before graduation. Anything left would be tossed."

"I was never told that," Sophie shrieked.

"Put the notice on every locker myself, Miss. It was there a week ago."

Sophie tried to remember what she was doing a week ago. Certainly she'd been down here, but she was too preoccupied with the upcoming celebration to pay any notice. But she was certain no notice was hanging on her locker. Nor did she remember them on anyone else's. Again, she was preoccupied. "Who cleaned out the lockers?"

"I did." He peered into the empty locker. "That's why I'm surprised to see you."

"Why is that?"

"Don't remember anything in yours." He scratched his head. "Must be getting senile."

"You remember it was empty?"

"Thought you'd cleaned it out yourself."

Sophie didn't, but someone else had. And she was sure she knew the culprit. Her father was looking at her strangely. Like he didn't believe her anymore. When the guard left, he scowled at her.

"I've had enough of your shenanigans."

"Daddy, I'm not lying."

"I come here to retrieve your work. As it turns out it's been conveniently tossed out."

"This isn't a prank. Someone took it."

"I've seen enough." He stomped up the stairs then turned when he reached the top. "You coming?"

"Not just yet. I'll see you back at the apartment."

"Don't tarry for too long."

"I won't." She slid down her locker and dissolved into tears.

Chapter Five

The first thing Raymond saw when he walked into the catacombs was a slouched silhouette. The figure was rumpled and quivering. Hoarse sobs filled the space echoing and rebounding off the walls. He rushed forward. Watery brown red-rimmed eyes looked up at him woefully bereft.

"Miss Noble, what's happened?" He knelt beside her. Not knowing what to do.

"It's all gone." Her shoulders shook, and another soul ripping cry escaped. "No one believes me."

"You best start from the beginning." He slid down next to her, patting her shoulder, which didn't have the calming affect desired. It only made her cry harder. He dug into his breast pocket and pulled out a handkerchief.

"Thank you." She took it and dabbed at her eyes. She sniffed. "I'd always imagined graduating to be some great big adventure. The last hurrah before you're sent off into the world to work and support yourself."

"That's one way to look at it. But I think it's a more serious event than you believe." He rubbed his forehead wondering how this naïve girl had managed to get this far in her life. Flitting around here and there. Never finding root. Although her attitude toward life was charming at times. Most certainly fun and amusing, it couldn't make up every moment like she seemed to expect.

"Now you tell me." She wailed again.

"I bet if you think back, you've been told that before."

"No." She shook her head. "No one warned me life could be this hard." She wiped her nose that was fast getting redder than a tomato.

"Then let me assure you," he chuckled. "Life can hit some very rough patches. How you get through them lets you know your character."

"Well." She hiccupped. "I already know my character. I'll forever be seen as a silly little girl. That's definitely not what I intended."

"There are worse things to be, Miss Noble."

"Like what?" She pulled her hair back, exposing a long supple neck. The kind he would like to nip if given half the chance. He grimaced. Not only was he not going to get that chance, but even having this kind of thought was inappropriate given his position in the art department. She turned her warm brown eyes on him. "I doubt you have ever had to make sacrifices."

"On the contrary." He almost whispered the words they were so painful to get out. "How about having no talent."

"What are you talking about?"

"I've seen your paintings. They are exquisite even if they are imitations of other artists' work. I don't have talent like that."

"But," her eyes grew wide. "You're an expert."

"Oh I know every nuance of every artist who ever existed. I can tell you about technique, choice of color, and if a painting is genuine. But I can't draw, sculpt, or paint."

"You can't be serious."

"I'm very serious."

"Then how did you get to be dean of the art department."

He shifted, trying to get a better position on the hard cement floor. There was none. "That's a long story and one I prefer not to get into right now. Why don't you tell me why you are here and crying?"

"I came here to get the rest of my paintings." She sniffed again. "It was the only way I could prove that I painted the Degas in class. But when I got here, everything was gone."

"These stalls get cleaned out at the end of every semester." Something that should have occurred to him when Overton made his offer. The man knew there would be nothing to see. And he'd let the bastard slip that one past him.

"So I've been told." She pointed her finger at the wall across from her. "But no one told me before it happened."

"And you think someone disposed of your paintings." Not as far off a notion as one would expect.

"Yes." She leaned her head into the chicken wire. Fresh tears streaming down her cheeks. "And now I can't prove anything."

"What about the paintings hanging at club 501?"

"You noticed?" Humor lit her watery eyes.

"Of course I did. Your little symbol didn't escape me."

She smiled, admiration flickered on her adorable face. "I'm afraid they won't be of much help. I painted them over the summer break. Uncle Harry loved them so much, he hung them in his club. But all they do is show I can paint a forgery. They can't implicate anyone else. I didn't paint those paintings to pass them off as genuine, but now I can't prove it."

"Then we'll have to find some other way."

"We?"

"Yes, we." He shot her a stern look. "As I'm sure you've already suspected, Overton is involved. But it takes more than one person to pull off this kind of scheme."

"What do you mean?"

"In order for this to work, Overton needed a forger." He shot her a pointed glance. "That would be you."

"That part I know."

"Then he would need a person who could forge a believable provenance. From the looks of the one on the Degas. He has that person too. Then he would need someone to pose as the owner and sell it to a gallery."

"I see." She was charming when lost in thought. "Do you have any notion who those people might be?"

"No, but I bet we can find out. I thought I might pay a visit to the man who owned the painting before Grayson."

"I'm coming with." She stood and brushed the dirt off her skirt.

"Why does that not surprise me?"

"Hey, I have a right to this information too." She jutted out her chin. Another adorable action.

"Fine." He had no idea why he was letting her tag along. Maybe if he kept an eye on her he could keep her out of trouble. Maybe. "But you have to promise that if things get dangerous, you will back off."

"I promise." Then she smiled, and his world brightened one hundred percent more. He'd better be careful, or he'd be eating crow. He had the suspicion he'd just bitten off more than he could chew. It wasn't like him, but he'd never felt better in his life.

****

"What makes you think Mr. Darton will even talk to us?" Sophie took long strides to keep up with Professor Critchton. "If he's in on it, I bet he doesn't even open the door."

"I don't know that he will," Professor Critchton didn't slow his pace. He was just as curious as she was about the forgery scheme. Her heart warmed at his interest. The man was not nearly as much of a stick in the mud as she originally thought. He'd turned out to be quite pleasant company. Made her wonder who else she'd misjudged so harshly. She had a lot more to learn about human nature. That did not bode well for her budding career drawing cartoons. Every nuance and characteristic of a person was exaggerated to expose a person's true nature. She couldn't even glean the personality of the dean. A very poor recommendation of her talents, indeed. "But we have to start somewhere."

They approached a tall wrought-iron fence intertwined with vines of some white, sweet-smelling flower. She inhaled deeply. It was such a pleasant fragrance she almost forgot her mission. Shaking her head clear, she followed Professor Critchton to the gate.

"Wow." With the exception of Grandmama's mausoleum of a residence she'd never seen a structure so large. It was so massive it could fit five houses inside it. It rose at least three floors high and took up as many lots. It was very grand with statues guarding picturesque gardens. Sophie bet there was even a hedge maze in the back. How did one go about living in such a place? Twenty people could live there comfortably and never see each other. "One person lives here?"

"We don't know that." Professor Critchton looked down at her with a quizzical glance. She guessed she was paying attention to the wrong details again. But she couldn't help it in the shadows of such a gargantuan house. No, it wasn't a house. More like a hotel. "All I know is that this is the address of the man who donated the Degas. From the looks of the place, a valuable painting could have been found in the attic."

Professor Critchton unlatched the gate. It squeaked open sounding like it hadn't been oiled in years. Intrigued, she trailed behind him taking in the beauty of the place. Birds chirped gaily in the tops of tall poplar trees. Welcoming rosebuds lined the walkway to the house. Someone cared a great deal about this property. The lawn was freshly mowed. The bushes well-manicured. There was even a topiary of a dolphin at the center of one of the gardens, charmingly ringed by petunias. The sound of water could be heard at a distance. There must be a fountain here somewhere, but she couldn't place where it was.

"This place is heavenly."

Professor Critchton's lips curved in an amused smile. It was like he viewed her as a child on a first trip to a grand park. Her lip jutted out at the thought. She quickly pulled it back. No need to give credence to his impression of her. If it was indeed his impression. The man was such a puzzle. Sophie was hard pressed to figure him out. They ascended the five steps to the front porch. The red brick was dotted with ivy. Bees hummed around the geraniums.

A door knocker in the shape of an angel hung in the middle of a solid oak door. Professor Critchton lifted it and let it fall with a reverberating thud. Sophie was full of jitters waiting to see who would open the door. She clutched her purse firmly against her stomach in a vain attempt to quell the butterflies dancing inside it. *Please let us get the answers we need.* After what seemed like eons, the door creaked open revealing an elderly man with wire rimmed glasses looking down his nose at her. Some things never change.

"May I help you?" the man drawled.

"Do I have the pleasure of addressing Mr. Darton?" Professor Critchton asked smoothly.

"No, sir." The man stood squarely in the doorway. Sophie tried to peer around his rotund belly and square shoulders to get a look inside. The man's massive physique blocked her view.

"Is Mr. Darton home?" Professor Critchton persisted.

"No one by that name lives here."

"What?" Sophie asked. The man's rheumy eyes turn to her. "Are you sure?"

"Of course, Miss." The man was not taken aback by her exclamation. In fact he sounded bored. Like he was dealing with a door-to-door salesman instead of visitors. "I have served this household for over fifty years."

"I see." Professor Critchton's fingers stroked his chin. "The problem is this address was supplied as the location where a valuable piece of art was found."

"It's the first I've heard of it, sir."

"Has a man named Darton ever lived here?"

"No, sir, this residence has been in the Borden family since it was built."

"Maybe this Darton chap is acquainted with the family?"

The man shook his head. "Impossible."

Sophie's spirits fell. She had to admire Professor Critchton's tenacity, but the man in the doorway was as cryptic as a vault with fifteen locks that'd been thrown into the ocean. She decided to emulate Professor Critchton and press on with the inquiry. "Why is that? He could be a neighbor."

"No, Miss. The only surviving member of the household is Miss Borden. She's been in the convalescent home for over three years. She has no visitors or family to speak of."

"Have you recently had any work done on the house?" Raymond persisted.

"Not that it is any of your business, but no."

"No one in the attic?"

"There has been no one in this house for years. Only a small staff keeps it in good condition. When the lady of the house passes, it's slated to be sold at auction."

"Would it be too much to hope Mr. Darton is a member of your staff?"

"It is."

"Friend of the staff?"

"Sir, I know no one by that name. I assure you, I am aware of all the staff's acquaintances. They know no one by that name. Now if you'll excuse me. You have taken up enough of my time."

The door closed with a terminal bang. "Well that was rude," Sophie sputtered.

"I'm surprised he talked to us this long. Maybe it was amusing given he doesn't see many people anymore."

"Maybe." They walked down the steps. "This is such a lovely place. It should have a family in it."

"It isn't surprising Darton chose this place. No one lives here to dispute his claim."

"I guess no one bothered to check the legitimacy of the address. If they had bothered to come here, the butler would have set them straight."

"Why would anyone check? How often does one give the wrong address when making such a generous donation?"

"Indeed." Sophie stopped and stared up at him. "We're back where we started with no idea where to look."

"Then let's start with what we know. How about we call on Overton."

"Don't think that will get us anywhere."

"Oh, ye of little faith." Professor Critchton winked. "He might reveal something by accident."

****

When they arrived at Professor Overton's office, the door was shut. Sophie's heart sunk. Maybe he wasn't in. That would put a pall on an already unproductive day. It made sense given the summer session wasn't due to begin for three weeks. "Has he taken vacation days?"

"Not that I'm aware of," Professor Critchton said. "But faculty are allowed to take off days. It's not like a normal job where you have to clock in. As long as he completes his course assignments, no one complains."

"Must be nice." Sophie poised to knock just to be certain he wasn't in. She halted mid-knock as heated voices emerged from within. Two male voices argued about something, but she couldn't make out the words through the solid wood door. She resisted the urge to lean her ear against the solid surface. Not only was Professor Critchton with her, her mother's voice wafted through her head admonishing her from doing so.

Professor Critchton leaned against the wall. "At least we know he's in."

"Then we will wait."

It was a good thing she wasn't leaning against the door because within seconds a man swung the door wide. "You'd better make sure nothing else is amiss. We can't afford any more delays."

Leaving the door open a crack, he plowed into Sophie. She stumbled back. Professor Critchton's strong hands steadied her from toppling to the floor.

"Sorry, Miss." The man doffed his hat. Sophie could do no more than nod. His face was beet red. Clearly in distress, he scuttled on. There was something vaguely familiar about him. She'd seen that tangle of red hair emerging from his hat before. But before she could halt his progress, he'd rushed into the stair well.

"That was interesting," Professor Critchton said close to her ear. His breath sent pleasant tingles jolting down her spine. She should move away knowing the way he made her feel was unseemly but couldn't bring herself to extricate from the peace of being near him.

"Is someone there?" Overton said from the back of his office.

"Yes, Overton, I need a word with you." Professor Critchton let go of her and strode into the room. The coldness left by his absence startled her. When had she become so accustomed to his presence? That wasn't important. Right now they needed information on what was happening to her paintings. She followed Professor Critchton inside.

Overton cleared his throat at Sophie's entrance. Not so pleased to see her, it seemed. In a few short days she'd gone from teacher's pet to vile intruder. Something was definitely up. Sophie sat in the chair next to Professor Critchton and waited for one of them to speak.

"What's this about?" Overton asked.

"I'm here about the Degas." Professor Critchton leaned forward with such ease.

"I thought we'd settled the matter." Professor Overton opened his desk drawer and slipped a piece of paper inside. He closed the drawer before Sophie could get a good look at it, but she could swear it was a note of some kind. One he didn't want anyone to see. That was promising. The only problem was there was no way to get to it without Overton noticing.

"Did you?" Professor Critchton steepled his fingers at his chin and looked at Overton for longer than was considered appropriate. Sophie guessed he was trying to feel Overton out. Overton shifted in his seat, discomfort wafting off of him like stale summer heat.

"Yes, in fact, I had." Overton's gaze shifted to Sophie then back to Professor Critchton. "I guess you are wanting to look in the catacombs."

"I've already done that. They're empty."

Overton smacked his hand against his forehead. "I forgot they're cleaned out after classes ended."

"Convenient, that," Professor Critchton said.

"About that," Sophie said. "How is it I wasn't notified that my locker was going to be cleared out?"

"I have no idea. Notice was posted on every stall. Maybe yours fell off."

"Still you knew I was concerned my work was being passed off as genuine. Don't you think it would be prudent to keep my art?"

"You think much too highly of yourself, Miss Noble." He leaned back in his chair. It creaked in protest. "Your artwork isn't worth squat."

"Really," Professor Critchton responded before Sophie could. "I've seen her work, and it's exquisite. Good enough to be passed off as an original."

"You can't believe her story. If you'll recall, this is the girl who set off fireworks endangering the students and their families."

"That may be. But unlike the matter of the Degas, her participation in that event has been dealt with."

Overton sputtered, turning an unappealing shade of crimson. He ran a finger through his collar. "I stand by my assessment that the Degas is genuine. It has been verified by a very reputable expert. I don't care how talented you think Miss Noble is, she isn't that good."

"I think she is."

"How can you be so sure?" The cocky expression had left his face to be replaced by a look of a man who could eat his own children.

"There is the small matter of the symbol just under the signature."

"What symbol?"

"The Celtic symbol I put on all my paintings." Sophie chimed in.

"That little doodle? An anomaly to be sure, but it doesn't mean she painted it." He thrust his finger at Sophie so hard if it'd been a knife it would have pierced her through the heart.

"Except I've seen that same symbol on the paintings that hang in her Uncle Harry's club."

"So?" He slammed his fist on the desk.

"They were purportedly painted by three different artists. That's a little hard to explain if her story wasn't true."

Sophie sat up straighter. Grateful that Professor Critchton was on her side.

"Good lord, you're besotted with this girl, aren't you?"

Sophie gasped. This man's insolence knew no bounds.

"I would be careful how you speak to me." Professor Critchton's guttural sound unnerved even her.

"Or what?" Overton stood palms in the center of his desk. "I'm tenured, you fool. You have no authority over me."

"Unless you're found guilty of a felony."

"I've heard enough. Get out of my office, now."

Professor Critchton rose.

"We're leaving?" Sophie asked surprised.

"There's nothing more we can accomplish here."

As they left the office and drifted down the hall without answers and at as much of a standstill as the day of the gala, a thought occurred to her. The man who'd been in the office before them. She was sure she'd seen him before. "Professor, have you ever seen that man who rushed past us earlier?"

"He didn't look familiar."

"He did to me. I'm sure I've seen him before."

"Where?"

It hit her like a flash. She'd been so intent on speaking to Overton, she'd almost forgotten the brash man. "David James!"

"That was David James? Are you certain?"

"Yes, he attended a session with our class this semester. Helping us with technique."

"I wonder why I've never seen him before now."

"How often do you get out of your office and look into the classrooms?"

"Not often enough, it seems."

"Anyhow, he held a contest to see which student had the best technique. I won that contest. And if I don't miss my guess, Mr. James gave him a note or Professor Overton jotted something down on that piece of paper he slid into his desk."

"Yes, I noticed that too. I guess we know where we're going next."

Sophie's spirits lifted. They left to hunt Mr. James down.

Chapter Six

"Don't you think we should get a taxi?" Sophie asked Professor Critchton as he turned the corner of the street. "The art supply shop is ten blocks from here, you know."

"Ten city blocks," he replied with a smile. "I thought you ladies liked walking."

"In a park. Not on streets filled with exhaust fumes." Wind rushed through her hair, threatening to lift her hat from her head. She grabbed the brim to hold it steady. Professor Critchton wasn't walking as fast as he did when they visited the Borden residence. He strolled beside her at a pace she could easily keep up with. That was an improvement at least.

"I thought it might give us a moment to talk," he said casually.

"What about?" She couldn't fathom what more information she could provide him. She'd already confessed to painting the forgeries. After that kind of declaration there wasn't much more to say.

"What possessed you to paint the forgeries anyhow?"

That was fair. Many talented artists excelled at what they did best without ever getting mixed up in a mess like this. "As I've said before, Professor Overton had us study the techniques of the great artists. It was his opinion that by imitating their techniques our own talents would emerge."

"While I can't disagree studying the techniques of other artists is a sound method of learning, usually the paintings don't carry the signature of the original artist. Yet I've seen four of your paintings that to the causal eye were painted by Degas, Renoir, Da Vinci, and Van Gough."

Sophie thought for a minute. What he said was true. Now that she thought about it, none of her classmates had signed the original artists name to their pieces. But their pieces never turned out as well as hers. "Professor Overton was so impressed with my work, he had me paint many pieces. To be honest, the signature started as a lark."

"Are you saying you signed the ballerina as Degas for a joke?" As politely as he was trying to say it, his voice was tinged with disgust.

Sophie sighed. "When you put it that way, it does seem stupid."

"I'll say."

"I wasn't trying to fool anyone. My symbol was below the signature every time."

He ran a hand through his thick brown hair. It occurred to her that she'd never seen him wear a hat like most gentlemen. Every time she saw him, he was dressed in a suit but never had a hat. "I'm not sure that was enough. That symbol has been overlooked two times already."

"In hindsight, I agree my actions were rather rash." Her gaze traveled to the sidewalk. Watching her feet take one step after the other was better than seeing the disappointment that surely resided in his brown eyes. "Professor Overton took such an interest in my work. I just got carried away with it all. It never occurred to me he would try to pawn them off as genuine."

"A fact he counted on, I'd wager."

Sophie hazarded a glance at his profile. His chin was firmly set. His eyebrows furrowed, and his mouth had taken a downward turn. But his irritation didn't appear to be directed at her. At least not that she noticed. Maybe that was because he wasn't looking at her but at a far-off point down the street. She followed the direction of his gaze but didn't detect anything out of the ordinary. One thing was certain, his opinion of her was more important than it had been a few days ago. She wanted him to like her. To see her as a grown woman and not just some silly girl.

"You think me naïve, don't you?"

He stopped and looked straight at her. "How else could something like this happen? I get that you didn't mean your paintings to be sold as the real thing, but for you to so willingly play into Overton's hands indicates a certain level of naivety."

So much for him seeing her as a grown woman. She couldn't think of anything she could say to dissuade him of his impression, and she didn't want to fight with him. He'd been kind enough to believe she wasn't actually knowingly part of the forgery ring. She shuddered to think how things might have turned out if he had. His belief in her innocence would have to be enough for now. "Fair enough."

They walked together in companionable silence for the next block. She couldn't get over how pleasant it was to be in his company. Not wanting to spoil the moment, she kept her mouth shut.

"What I don't get is how the experts were fooled. There are chemical tests that can be done on a new piece of work to authenticate it."

"That I can't help you with."

He eyed her skeptically. "Let me explain a little. The paint used a century ago is much different in makeup than that which is used today. Where did you get your supplies?"

"Overton provided all the canvases." She thought some more. "In the beginning, we bought our own supplies. However, after Mr. James's contest, I used the paints he gave me as first prize."

"Really?" Raymond pursed his lips, and a dimple emerged in the cleft of his chin. "Let me make sure I've got this straight. He gave you canvases, and you won the paints."

"Right."

"That means he could have treated the canvas with something, and the paints may have had the chemical content he needed."

"Hmmm."

"When were you gifted with these paints?"

"Before I painted the forgeries."

"That makes things a little clearer."

"What are you thinking?" Not sure she was grasping the full detail. Overton had given her treated canvases, and Mr. James gave her special paints. That she understood.

"Where else do you get supplies?" He favored her with a lopsided smile.

"That's how Mr. James is involved."

"Exactly. I think he's been mixing your paints and treating the canvases."

She stopped. "How do we prove that?"

He stood in front of her. "That's why we're about to go rattle his cage. Hopefully we'll get more out of him than Overton."

"Why are you helping me?"

"The reputation of the school for one." He took hold of her gloved hand. "And you have a great talent that shouldn't go to waste."

"What do you mean?"

"Miss Noble, anyone who can paint like you do shouldn't sell herself short by creating another artist's work. You have the ability to paint pieces with your own flair."

"Just because I can copy someone else's style doesn't mean I have any of my own. I'm good at cartoons, nothing more."

He frowned. "Quit selling yourself short. I know talent when I see it."

"Why does it matter to you what I do?"

"Because I've seen talent go to waste. It happened to my mother. I don't want it to happen to you."

She wasn't sure being compared to his mother was a good thing, but he had a far-off gaze tinged with such sadness that she couldn't help but inquire. "What happened to your mother?"

"She got quite a reputation for painting fairies and far-off lands. Then we found her talking to people who weren't there. She told us not to stand certain places or that we were blocking her view of a rainbow or pot of gold."

"Oh." That could not have been fun living with a mother who only saw a fantasy world. The past few days she'd been mad at her mother for only wanting her daughter to live a decent life. Professor Critchton didn't have a mother present enough to wish that for him.

"She was diagnosed with schizophrenia. I hate admitting this. My father locked her away. When she got better, she'd come home and go off medication. She'd paint again but then had more nervous breakdowns. Finally she had an operation, and all the light left her eyes."

"How horrible. I'm sorry you and your mother had to go through that."

"Thank you. Now can you see how precious your talent is and how you shouldn't throw it away?"

"I'm a cartoonist. There's nothing shameful about that."

"Cartoons are too fleeting. They're here one minute and gone the next. You're capable of so much more. You can create pieces that will last the test of time."

She knew he was trying to be supportive, but his attitude rankled. Creating cartoons was legitimate art whether he believed it or not. They saw things so differently. It was a shame too because she was really beginning to like him.

****

The bell on the door jangled when they entered the shop. Sophie waltzed inside as if she owned the joint. A woman really in her element. She inhaled deeply as she surveyed her surroundings.

The smell of oil paints, chalk dust, and pastels reminded Raymond of his mother's workroom. He used to sit and watch her paint. She would smile at him as she worked as long as he didn't sit on an elf or leprechaun or disturb their magic mushroom circle.

Her anger never scared him like it did his father. Everything she saw was put in her paintings and shared with Raymond. After the surgery, she was never the same. Not sad but empty just the same. He would never forgive his father for doing that to her. With one swish of his signature, the life went out of her.

He shook his head and pulled himself into the present. No use in dwelling on the things that couldn't be changed. He perused the items offered for sale. All prepackaged items. Boxes of pencils, crayons, and paints. Nothing individually made.

He picked up a carton of paints, making a show of examining them while Sophie went to speak with Mr. James.

"Hello Mr. James," she said brightly. "I was wondering if you could assist me in selecting the right colored pencils."

"I'll do my best, Miss." Mr. James glanced at her sideways as if trying to place her. Apparently he didn't get a good enough look at her when he rushed past her earlier today. One of the reasons she and Raymond separated once they entered the store. The other was to give Raymond time to examine the place.

"Wonderful!" She clapped her hands really laying it on thick. Raymond chuckled. The man seemed to eat it up. "I'm a cartoonist, and I need the exact right pencils for detailed shading."

"Right this way. Let me show you what we have."

Sophie followed him to the other side of the store. "The Axis brand is used by many professional cartoonists. They don't have the waxy residue that impedes outlining with ink."

"I see." The way her eyes brightened as she held the box was adorable. Her lips turned up in what could only be joy. She was mesmerized. He'd never really taken a good look at her cartoons. The only day he had he was distracted by her caricature of him. It was disappointing she saw him as such a dour individual. It wasn't as if he were some old codger ready to be put out to pasture. He was barely older than she. He knew she didn't like his disdain for her chosen medium. But it was his job to encourage pupils to reach their full potential. She was capable of so much more than working at a magazine or newspaper penning political cartoons. However, he might be a little too harsh to dismiss her passion so quickly. He resolved to take her art more seriously from now on.

"A new item that has become very popular is this little beauty." Mr. James handed Sophie another box. "When water is applied to drawings made with these pencils, it becomes like watercolors. That way, shading is a little more detailed. You can smooth a section lighter or darker with a paintbrush."

"How fascinating," she squealed.

Assured Sophie had his full attention, Raymond made his way to the back of the store. The backroom was covered by flimsy curtains that swayed with the slight air circulating around the room. He peered through the gap but only saw stacks of cartons. Needing to get a good look inside, he pulled the curtain aside ready to slip through. Overton blocked his way.

"Critchton, what are you doing here?"

"I could ask the same of you."

"It's no secret I buy all my art supplies here." His eyes narrowed. "I can't say I've ever seen you here."

"What difference does that make?"

"I'm sure I don't know." He examined his nails like they were the most interesting objects in the whole world. "But I am sure you don't belong behind this curtain."

"Not that I need to explain myself to you, but I was looking for a particular type of paint that wasn't out in the display. Since the shopkeeper was occupied, I thought I'd take a look in the back."

"Mr. James doesn't let anyone in the back."

"He let you back there."

"I'm a longtime customer. Maybe I could help you find what you need."

It was clear he wasn't going to get anywhere while Overton was in the shop. "No thanks, I'll come back later."

Sophie made her purchase and met him outside.

"Was that Overton?"

"Yes it was, and guess where I found him?"

"Where?"

"Emerging from the back room. I wonder if that is where your paintings are."

She put a finger to her chin. "If they are, it's a certainty they'll be moved after today. But where?"

Raymond's blood boiled. "Everywhere we go, we hit a dead end."

"We have to figure this out. My reputation is at stake."

He shot her a sidelong glance. "Only because you told everyone you'd painted forgeries."

Her eyes grew wide. "What was I supposed to do, let them sell my art at a profit it doesn't deserve? Dupe everyone into thinking new art had been discovered? That's just not right."

"But no one else seems to be on to them. Very few people believe you. We have to figure out a way to convince everyone that you created those paintings."

****

"What were they doing in my store?"

"I'm sure I don't know," Overton said. It seemed he'd be tailed everywhere he went. Unless he diverted attention from him onto someone else. He examined James, whose fingers trembled as he flipped the shop sign from open to closed. James turned toward him, his weak pale-blue eyes shimmering with worry.

"They haven't made the connection, have they?"

"Come now, David." He drummed his fingers on the counter. "Everyone who's anyone buys their art supplies here. What connection is there to make?"

"No one can know."

"No one does."

"I should never have mixed those paints for you. I'm through with this business. As soon as we unload those last paintings, I'm done."

"That's perfectly fine. I doubt we'll luck into another student with the same talents as Sophie Noble. Or someone that naïve. What a perfect blend that creature was."

"Well, it looks like she's gotten wise."

"Only because we were unfortunate enough that recluse Grayson decided to exhibit his collection." He patted James on the shoulder. "Relax. She'll be gone soon, and we can carry on where we left off."

"But what if someone believes her?"

"The only one who does is Critchton. Not even Miss Noble's family believes her. She's played too many pranks to be taken seriously. Remember the fireworks."

"That was her?"

"It was. If I'd had my way, she would have been expelled in disgrace. But Critchton got in the way of that. The man that took away my job. A man who isn't even an artist himself lording over me. Who the hell does he think he is anyway?"

"That's unfortunate, sir."

"It is. But maybe I can turn their hunt for the paintings to my advantage. Maybe I can disgrace him enough that he'll have to leave the university in embarrassment."

"That's a good plan, sir."

"It sure is." He chortled. The more he thought about it, the better the idea became. Maybe he could find a way to oust him. It was worth a try. Anything that got the heat off of him and his forgery ring.

****

"Sophie, wake up." Maddie shook her shoulders ousting her from a very nice dream. She rolled over refusing to waken. She was walking in the park with Raymond, her arm curled in his. They were laughing and talking when he pulled her in for a kiss. His lips were soft and warm, sending searing heat all the way to her toes. That's what a kiss should feel like, not like those bland, wet kisses from Peter. Raymond's kisses were filled with passion and ardor. At least in her imagination. Her eyes shot open.

"Maddie?" She rubbed her eyes.

"You will not believe the rumor I just heard." Maddie sat on the edge of the bed without ceremony pulling off her gloves. "Or more accurately, read in the gossip column in the paper."

"I'm listening."

"There's a rumor that you and Professor Critchton have been having an affair for months now. That the only reason you've been successful in the art program is because Critchton is so besotted with you that he insists the school ignore your shortcomings."

"That's not true." Sophie sat up straight almost bumping her head into Maddie's. Tawdry dreams aside, there hadn't been a moment's impropriety between the two of them. Maybe a few close calls, but nothing that couldn't be printed in the paper the next day. She burned at the insinuation she was loose and untalented. The nerve!

"Who would spread such a lie?" Maddie rested her chin on her hands. "I bet the school pays attention and Professor Critchton is going to have to meet with the administration."

"Oh no." Sophie's hand flew to her mouth. This had to be Overton attempting to deflect attention from him. But why bother? No one except Critchton believed her anyhow. That must be what he was trying to do. Alienate her only supporter. "I've made such a mess of things."

"Is there anything to this rumor?"

"You know there isn't." She fell back on the bed, her hands covering her eyes.

"As to your artistic skills, no doubt." Maddie's eyes gleamed with misplaced amusement. "But I've seen the way you look at him."

"I don't look at him in any particular way." Sophie peered at her through her fingers.

"Oh yes you do. I saw how you tried to avoid him at the MET. How you leaned into him at the gala. You like him."

"I do not!" Except Sophie suspected Maddie was right. She'd been enjoying herself too much when she was with him. Now he'd never speak to her again. How else was he going to keep his job? Student/teacher relationships were frowned upon. It appeared not to matter that she was to graduate in a matter of days. And they weren't even seeing each other.

"He's been helping me try to find the person behind the forgery scheme."

"Really?" Maddie exclaimed. "And this is the first time you've told me?"

"Sorry, after that fiasco at the gala, I wasn't sure you really believed me."

"Who cares about that? It's a caper, and that's good enough for me." She squared her shoulders and looked at her expectantly. "How can I help?"

"I'm not sure you can." She rubbed her forehead. "How did a class project become such a mess?"

"Because nefarious people saw your talent and took advantage of it." Maddie patted her free hand. "Now we need to figure out how to turn the tables on them."

"That's the problem. I have no proof this is going on. It's only my word. I have such a reputation as a prankster, no one believes me."

"Except Critchton." Maddie arched her brow.

"And now his job is in jeopardy because of me," Sophie said. "He may never speak to me again."

"I thought you didn't care."

"I don't." Sophie sat up smoothing out her nightgown. "It's just that he was the only one that was helping me."

"Well you've got me now. Fill me in."

"We think Overton was hiding my paintings at James' art store. But they discovered us there, and I think he may have moved them."

"Let me go look into that."

"Okay," Sophie said doubtfully. "The last time I was in Overton's office, he tried to hide a note. I'll try and track that note down."

Chapter Seven

For the umpteenth time this week she entered the art school. At this rate, she would be here more often than she was when classes were in session. Not the best recommendation for an artist. She should be out painting seascapes at Martha's Vineyard like when she was younger. Maybe in a park people-watching and sketching. Not here in this dusty corridor chasing down an old husk of a man.

As she rounded the corner, angry voices flew down the hallway. She slipped back around the corner and wedged herself against the wall. Her heart thundered in her chest as the men in the office argued. There were three of them. Two she recognized. Professor Overton's entitled raspy voice. Art store guy's desperate nasal shout. If you could call it that. Then a loud, full, rich baritone she didn't recognize. Both men shut up when he spoke like they hung on his every word. She imagined them craning their necks just to be closer to his words. She peered around the corner hoping to catch a glimpse of the unknown man, but all she could see were shadows shimmering along the back wall.

"You had better be sure this will work," the unknown voice said. "You've caused enough trouble with this one."

"How was I supposed to know the girl would see her work at the MET?" Overton sputtered. "That was not my sloppy work."

"N-n-no one thought that painting would be on display so soon," Mr. James said. "Most collectors want to keep their new acquisition to themselves for a time."

"Well aren't we lucky you found the one that was into sharing," the unknown man said. "Then to top it all off one of her blasted paintings ended up in the university exhibit."

"A coincidence," Overton said.

"I don't believe in coincidences. Something is up. If it weren't for the millions we stand to make, I would be done. There better not be another screwup."

"I assure you sure," Mr. James said. "There won't be any more missteps."

"True." Overton chuckled. "I've made sure the girl and dean will be chasing their tails with all the scandal regarding their relationship."

Sophie turned cold. It wasn't as if she didn't know the bastard had leaked a rumor on purpose. But the certainty in his voice gave her pause. He was hellbent on destroying her before she could set the record straight. And he was close too. She was running out of time.

The office door opened wider, and a large man emerged followed by Mr. James. Sophie tried to get a look at the stranger but could get no clear view due to Mr. James mincing behind him. Mr. James was thin but towered over the strange man. They disappeared down the staircase. She didn't dare attempt to follow. Overton was still in his office, and the door was open. She waited a few minutes, then Overton's bald head emerged followed by the rest of him. He shut the door and sauntered down the hall. The keys chained to his trousers jingled as he moved away.

This was her chance and blast it he had closed the door. Inhaling deeply, she peered around the corner. No sign of Overton or anyone else. She slinked up to the door and tried the knob. To her delight it turned, and the door swung open. Leave it to that pompous windbag to be so sure of himself he felt no need to lock the door. She slipped inside and went straight to the desk drawer. With a quick flick of her wrist she opened it. The piece of paper lay just inside. She snatched it up, elated she had found the missing information.

This detective work was easy. Almost too easy. It was definitely time to leave.

"Where do you think you're going?" Overton stuck his bulbous head in the door, a twisted smile on his beet red face. Sophie took a step back, clutching her newly found prize to her chest. "Don't look so surprised, dearie. I saw how you noticed that paper the other day and had a feeling you might come snooping around."

Sophie's heart lurched. The room grew dim, and it was hard to breathe. How could she be so stupid? Of course a man as crafty as Overton wouldn't be so careless as to leave his door open. "How did you know I would be here right now?"

"I didn't. But I prepared for the occasion that you would appear." He stalked toward her. "Now give me that."

"No." She clutched the slip of paper tighter and attempted to ease around him. His girth blocked her way around his desk. She looked over his shoulder desperate for anyone to walk by, but the hall was as empty as a deep cavern in a cave. She had to get away. She screamed.

Overton covered her mouth. "Quiet, girl, your screech is irritating and there's no one to hear you scream."

Her heart sank at the truth in his words. No one to save her. No knight in shining armor would rescue her from her predicament. Well, she had gotten herself into this, and she would bloody well get herself out of it. She opened her mouth and bit down. Overton howled shaking his wounded hand. "You bitch!"

Sophie spit out the metallic taste of blood and dug her heel into the side of his foot. But instead of having the crippling effect she desired, his face turned crimson and purple. He grabbed her arm and yanked her through the door. "That's enough out of you."

She squirmed. Then dug her heels into the floor, leaving black heel marks along the floor. He opened a door on the opposite end of the hall and shoved her in. She stumbled inside. The smell of antiseptic and ammonia choked her. She whirled around and rushed at the door. Overton slammed the door closed, cutting off all source of light. She tried the knob. Locked. She pounded on the door. "Let me out."

"Don't worry, my dear." Overton chuckled. "You won't be in there forever. They'll find you eventually and let you out. But not before your reputation is shot and that special friend of yours is ruined."

"No, you can't do this." Sophie slid down the door sobbing.

"It's already done. I'm sorry I can't stick around to see the chaos, but I have some art to sell and a plane to catch."

She coughed in the darkness, clawing at the wall and the door. She tipped over the stuff on the shelves looking for something to pry the door open to no avail. After a long while of gagging and drifting, there was a rustle at the door. Sophie turned with hope. "Who's there?"

"It's me," Maddie whispered. "What are you doing in there?"

"Overton locked me inside."

"Well clever girl leaving your heel marks on the floor."

"Never mind that. Can you get me out?"

The rattle of the knob. "No, I have no key. I'm going to get help. Sit tight."

****

Ray Critchton sat at his desk mulling over the fix he was in. It was all over the papers. Now he would have to explain himself. The worst part was he couldn't deny it. He loved Sophie. A soft rap at his door brought him out of his reverie. He strode into the outer office and opened the door. A woman with soft brown hair stood before him.

"Are you Professor Crichton?" she said in a breathy voice.

"Yes."

"I'm Maddie. I—I mean we need your help."

"I'm sorry?"

"Sophie is locked in a broom closet, and we need the key."

He grabbed his coat off the rack and slipped it on. He followed Maddie down the hall. "How the devil did Sophie get locked in a broom closet?"

"She was running down a clue, and Overton shoved her in."

"What?" He raced a hand through his hair. "That woman will never learn. How can she be so reckless?"

Maddie shot him a rueful glance. "Are you joking? She thrives on recklessness."

"Well, let's get her out of there."

They reached the closet. He fished in his pocket for the keys.

"Sophie?" Maddie said. "We're here, are you all right?"

"Yes, just hurry. I can't wait to get out of here."

Crichton opened the door. Sophie flew out and right into Maddie's arm. "Thank you, thank you, thank you."

Ray squelched the disappointment that Sophie didn't choose him to thank in such a fashion. Clearly the two were friends. Had probably known each other all their lives. "What did you think you were doing?"

"I was trying to find the slip of paper that Overton stashed in the desk the other day."

Maddie pulled her to arm's length. "Did you find it?"

"Yes, but Overton got it back. I didn't even get a chance to look at it to see what it said." Sophie rubbed her eyes and sighed. "Now we'll never know what he was planning."

"I think I can help with that." Maddie said. "I followed that art guy to a large warehouse. I think that's where they keep the artwork. That's what I came here to tell you." She reached into her purse and pulled out a slip of paper. "Here is the address."

She looked to Critchton and then Sophie. That mischievous gleam was back. "Looks like you two have things well in hand. I will inform the Bobbies about everything while you head to the warehouse."

****

The warehouse was a massive structure on the corner of an isolated street. With the exception of an errant scrap of paper blowing in the breeze, nothing stirred. From all appearances no one was here, but the sliding door was pulled back an inch. Either the building was abandoned or someone had opened the door. Sophie had to admit it was the perfect out-of-the-way place to stash the forgeries.

Critchton and Sophie inched along the side wall, its metal surface gleaming in the evening sunset. They peered into the tiny opening. A huge empty space yawned back. Sunlight streamed through the windows that lined each wall like a spotlight onto the cement floor. Nothing! Just a cavernous, musty room.

"This can't be right. I was so sure we'd find Professor Overton here." Sophie's insides twisted. They had to find and stop him before it was too late. "Where is everything?"

"Maybe we're not in the right place."

"No. This is the address Maddie gave us."

"She could be wrong about the reason Mr. James was here."

"Why else would he be here? This place is huge."

"Wait." Raymond pointed. "I see a staircase at the other end."

Sophie glanced in the direction Raymond indicated. A metal stair cloaked in shadows loomed at the back corner of the warehouse. She clapped her hands together. "Oh, there's another floor."

Ray eased the door back a little farther. Sophie flinched at the screech his efforts emitted. The sound rebounded against the walls, echoing through the emptiness. If Overton was here, he'd surely be alerted. Once inside she heard a scraping noise like someone was dragging something heavy along the upper floor. Sophie and Raymond looked at each other. A deep frown creased his brow. She imagined she wore the same expression.

"Do you think he's packing my paintings?"

Raymond shook his head. "No, I don't think he'd want to damage them by dragging them along a cement floor. Plus your paintings aren't that heavy."

"Then what's he doing?"

"Let's see what's going on, shall we?"

She followed Raymond up the stairs not sure what they would find. But from the sound of it, it wasn't good. Her stomach churned. What if they were too late? The top floor wasn't as large as the bottom. At the far end of the room were windowpanes filtering the room with the rays of the setting sun. On the right side of the room, her paintings were lined against the wall. She almost clapped in glee. Movement at the far corner caught her attention.

"How did you find me?" Overton froze, his hand gripped around a canvas wrapped around something bulky. Then her heart sank. She didn't want to know what was inside the material. It was too large and uneven to be a painting.

"That isn't important." Raymond crossed his arms. "Maybe you should tell us what's going on."

"None of your business." Overton had a sickly pallor to his ruddy complexion hidden under a sheen of pasty white. Sophie's gaze traveled to the sack sagging on the floor. She wasn't sure but the outline of the bag looked like a body. Overton turned his back, revealing the bulge of a gun. Her heart hammered a warning.

"Sophie, stay behind me." Raymond swept a protective arm, scooping her so he stood in front of her blocking her view. She peeked around his shoulders. Overton dropped the canvas. It hit the floor with a thud. An arm draped out of the opening.

"Oh no." Sophie's hands flew to her mouth, a scream stuck in her throat. "What have you done?"

"What had to be done. James wasn't as comfortable with our arrangement. He had to be eliminated."

"You won't get away with this. The police are on their way," Sophie said.

"I doubt that." He trailed a finger along the frames. "You fancy yourself a little detective. You two wouldn't be here on your own if the police were on their way."

He stalked toward them.

"Stop this, Overton. This is madness," Critchton said.

"Not by a long shot." He shoved Sophie out of the way. He punched Critchton. Critchton fell against some crates sending a box cutter skittering across the floor. Sophie screamed. "What a wimp of a boyfriend you've got there. That was very satisfying."

"Professor Critchton is more a man than you'll ever be. You just caught him by surprise."

She should run to get help, but she couldn't leave Critchton. "You won't get away with this."

"I already have. The buyers are coming soon." He approached. She backed away. He grabbed her. "Maybe it's better that you're here after all."

"Get away from her." Critchton pulled off the floor. He ran for her.

"I wouldn't do that if I were you." He pulled her against him and held the gun against her temple. "One more move, and I shoot her."

He pulled Sophie out onto the roof, backing up to the very edge. His arm curled around her neck choking off air. She clawed at his sleeve trying to relieve the pressure. She kicked at his calf. His hold loosened. She breathed in a mouthful of oxygen. "I would settle down, missy. No matter how hard you fight I will pin all this on you."

"How do you plan to do that?" Raymond inched forward holding a box cutter.

"You've always been such a pain in the ass," Overton spat. "I should have had your job. Then none of my operation would have been revealed. Maybe I should just kill you now."

Overton leveled the gun on Critchton. All Raymond had was a box cutter. Sophie had to do something. Sophie stomped on Overton's instep digging her heel deep. She wasn't sure how much he would feel underneath his leather soles but maybe it would distract him enough to take his attention off Raymond.

Overton stumbled. The gun went flying. Sophie took her opportunity and shoved backward. They toppled on the edge. His arm pulled her with him. My God! They were going to plummet to the ground. Sophie caught a view of the pavement. She struggled to get free. Strong hands gripped her and pulled her back to the roof. Raymond caught Overton's foot.

"Don't let me fall!" Overton screamed.

"Quit struggling." Raymond said, his voice calmer than Sophie could imagine. She shook against the wall watching the scene. "Sophie, I need your help. Grab his other leg."

With speed she didn't know she possessed, she raced to the other side of Overton. She grabbed his pants. They tore under the strain. She grabbed the exposed flesh, but it slipped through her sweaty palms. His leg hung in the air flailing. She reached for it again.

"Hurry, Sophie, his shoe is slipping off."

In horrible slow motion she grasped his free leg as his shoe fell to the pavement. His leg shifted an inch. She held on as tightly as she could. But it wouldn't be enough. She hung on the edge of the building, sliding over the edge.

"Overton, give me your hand."

The man she had seen as a mentor only days ago lifted his hand to Raymond. At the same time, Sophie lost hold of Overton. He reached desperately for a handhold but was unable to clasp onto Raymond. He plummeted downward, his screech of terror the only thing that reached them before he hit the ground.

Sophie closed her eyes at the impact and slid down the wall shaking uncontrollably. "What have I done?"

Despite her best efforts, she'd cost a man his life. Raymond gathered her up in his arms. "Nothing. He did this to himself. We did the best we could."

"It wasn't good enough," she sobbed.

Two uniformed officers walked onto the rooftop. "Stand with your hands up."

They rose lifting their hands into the air.

"Officers, there's been an accident."

One of the officers nodded toward the upstairs room. "Doesn't much look like an accident to me."

"Professor Overton killed that man. His gun is over there." The officer's eyes traveled where Raymond indicated. "You'll find Professor Overton's body on the ground."

"We need you to come down to the station until we sort things out."

****

With as much enthusiasm as she could muster, Sophie stepped into Club 501. A place as familiar to her as her own home. Uncle Harry and Aunt Meggie had outdone themselves. The room decorated with fairy lights and gossamer lit on every ballgown within reach including hers. Sophie's long skirt made of tulle and satin swooshed with every step. It was the evening she had been anticipating for weeks. The celebration of her crowning achievement. Her graduation party. But nothing right down to the lovely rose centerpieces on every table could lift her spirits.

After the chaos had died down, the police had released Raymond and her. She had been cleared of all wrongdoing, but that would never erase Overton's screams. She would replay that event over and over until the day she died. Nothing could erase the shame of allowing Overton to die. No matter how many times Raymond told her otherwise she would always believe there was something they could have done differently.

Her parents were still ready to ship her off and sentence her to London where she would be paraded around like a prize thoroughbred. Overseen by her overbearing Grandmama. Mother's own experiences should have dissuaded her from that action, but she seemed pleased she would be rid of Sophie. Maybe she deserved it. If she had been more observant and dutiful, she wouldn't have gotten caught up in this mess.

She sighed, pulling all the resolve she had to get through this evening. Clutching her sketch pad, she walked to the table reserved for her family. Fortunately, they were absent at the moment. Grateful for the solitude, Sophie sunk into her chair and opened her sketch book. At least she would always have her art. Pulling off her gloves she grabbed her charcoal. The room was so pretty. It would be a shame not to memorialize the view.

"What are you doing?" A soft hand patted her shoulder causing her to jump. "This is your graduation party and you're going to celebrate."

Sophie looked up to see good old unflappable Maddie. If only she could be as stalwart as she. But she didn't have the problems Sophie did.

"Yeah," Iris said over Maddie's shoulder. "This party is in your honor."

"I don't feel like celebrating."

"What's the matter?" they said in unison. Each took a seat beside her, Maddie patting her shoulder, Iris looking on with concern.

"The last few weeks have been hell." Too tired to keep the melodrama out of her voice Sophie sighed heavily. "I'm afraid my parents are going to ship me to London."

"Why?" Iris asked.

"That's not so terrible. I'll be there," Maddie said, exasperation creeping into her voice. Sophie would have to be careful how she formed the next words. The last thing she needed was to insult another dear friend. Just like that, the tears fell, dripping down her cheeks like a waterfall. She couldn't stop them. Iris handed Sophie a handkerchief. She dabbed her eyes.

"I'm sorry, Maddie. It's just that I wasn't prepared to go to London. My life and career are here. I've just made such a mess of things."

"That's okay," she said still patting Sophie's shoulder. "Let it out. But you really shouldn't fuss so. I've already invited Audra to visit London. We could really make a party of it."

Also, there could be some drama.

Iris jumped up. "Audra. Have either one of you seen her?"

Sophie's gaze followed Maddie's glance over her shoulder to the bar. "Not yet."

"Oh my God," Iris cried. "She promised she wouldn't take too long. Something must have happened." She rose and wormed her way through the crowd in the direction where Uncle Harry and Aunt Meggie stood.

"What is it, Soph?" Maddie's concern sent another bout of tears coursing down her cheeks.

Sophie swiped at the tears taking a few minutes to gather her wits about her. Then it all poured out of her like a torrent. "My parents were bleeding mad about my part in the forgeries. I tried to explain I hadn't meant for that to happen. Then when Overton died they were distressed by my involvement in that event. Even though I've been cleared, they keep telling me this is not how well-behaved ladies act. "

"I see," Maddie said. "Maybe going abroad isn't such a bad thing. Think of your reputation. At least you won't have people staring at you."

"I don't care what people think."

"Well, no matter what people think of you, your parents have your best interests at heart," Maddie said.

"I know. It's just that I viewed my life so differently. Nothing has turned out as I planned." Sophie wiped her nose. "I'm just not sure what to do anymore."

"If you don't want to go to London, we'll just have to figure out a different plan," Maddie said.

Laughter bubbled up from Sophie unbidden. Hadn't she been trying to do just that? Maddie joined in. For a moment, things were just the same as always. Just two friends chatting and laughing about their adventures. But her life had become a lot more serious than when they gallivanted about Martha 's Vineyard as girls. They were grown up now. All of them venturing toward their future looming in front of them just out of reach.

Sophie said, "All I've ever wanted was to create cartoons for a newspaper. Remember the adventures I used to write about us?"

"You are much better than that now," Maddie agreed. "You should aim much higher than that."

"I don't know." Sophie sunk in her chair. "The caricatures come so easy. They don't take as long as an oil painting."

"Nothing worthwhile is ever easy," Maddie said.

They were veering into dangerous territory. Not an area Sophie wanted to discuss at the moment. She looked around for something else to talk about.

Something that had nothing to do with her. Uncle Harry and Aunt Meggie stood at the bar sipping champagne in solitude. Not mingling with the crowd as usual. Iris headed back to the table with an odd, twisted grimace on her face. She slumped down in her chair and rested her chin on her hand. Her mood much murkier than before. "What's going on?" Sophie asked. "Where's Audra?"

"She left the party." Iris's face hardened, and an uncharacteristically steely tone tinged her voice. Like she was put out with Audra. What was that about? It was as if the whole world went topsy turvy in twenty-four hours.

"Am I missing something?"

"It's nothing." Iris sniffed. "Let's get back to you. What were you saying?"

It seemed she wouldn't escape this conversation. But she didn't have to talk about London. She slapped her hand on the table. "Girls, I neglected to mention the weirdest thing."

"What?" they said.

"Peter asked me to marry him at the art gala."

"What?" Their eyes grew wide.

Sophie took a deep breath to be heard over the music. "I said Peter asked me to marry him." Abruptly the music stopped. To her horror, her voice carried about the room. All eyes fell on her. Heat crept into her cheeks. She couldn't do anything right today. She peered around the room to see if anyone important heard the damning statement.

"Really?" Maddie's eyes grew bright, not even taking notice of the people gawking at their table. Sophie breathed deeply hoping for the interest in her little neck of the world to pass. Blessedly, the orchestra struck up another ballad and attention turned to interests other than her.

"Oh, tell us everything." Iris clasped her hands together.

"I said no. He tried to kiss me to convince me I was wrong. Raymond had to rescue me."

"Oh." They both shrunk lower in their chairs.

"I don't love him." Sophie didn't know why she was trying to justify herself to them, but she needed to explain. "There was no spark when I was with him. We were just good chums. Now we're not even that."

"How awful," Maddie said.

"He didn't act like a gentleman," Iris said with conviction.

"What's this?" Maddie pulled Sophie's sketch from the table. "Oh, now he's cute!"

"Let me see." Iris snatched her drawing before Sophie had a chance to retrieve it. "He's dreamy. If I don't miss my guess this is Raymond Critchton. I thought you liked him."

"I drew that a long time ago. I should have destroyed it." After all she and Raymond had been through, her caricature was way off the mark. How could she have been so uncharitable?

"Well." Maddie peered at the drawing more closely. "Aside from the length of his nose and his snobby look, which I'm sure is done for effect, he has a pleasant turn of the mouth. He has a full head of hair and soft brown eyes."

Sophie snatched the drawing away. Then she really looked at it. As unkind as she'd been about the length of his nose, she didn't realize she'd captured his broad, masculine shoulders. He really did have an attractive shape. And there was a glimmer of kindness in his eyes. Not to mention his full, kissable lips. She didn't like her friends mooning over him. Acid simmered in her belly over her friends' giggles about his physique.

"So you definitely have changed your opinion?" Maddie asked fixing her with a penetrating stare.

"Maybe." She shrugged. "I drew this because I was mad at him. He's always so judgmental. Always looking to find fault. But he's actually not like that. He is very kind."

"So, then, you like him." Iris beamed.

"I don't know." Sophie couldn't shake the disappointment that she hadn't seen him since that awful day on the warehouse rooftop.

"Isn't that him looking at Uncle Harry's art collection?"

"What?" Sophie peered over at the wall that held three of her paintings. The fakes of famous artists. Uncle Harry loved the buzz those painting stirred. It was all in fun and not hurting anyone. Critchton was examining them. Her heart sped up at the sight of his broad shoulders and commanding stance. He really was quite attractive.

"I didn't know he was here." Sophie tried to keep the squeal of delight from her voice.

"Maybe he's here to congratulate you." Maddie glanced in his direction. "I heard my Aunt Jessie speaking to someone on the matter of your employment with a newspaper."

"Hey." Iris grabbed Sophie's arm. "Maybe you should go talk to him."

"Hmmm." Sophie jumped out of the chair. "Maybe I should."

Sophie grabbed her glass of champagne and headed in Raymond's direction. Smoothing her skirts attempting to settle her nerves. Casually as she could manage, she strolled over to him as he leaned close to each painting. Looking them up and down inch by precious inch. It was hard to tell. He looked one over then went to the next one and back to the one before. He definitely seemed perplexed. Sophie didn't hold any illusions she was that good. Especially when she painted these pictures.

"See anything you like?" Sophie sidled up next to him all innocence and grace. His gaze turned to her.

"Ah, Miss Noble, you look splendid tonight."

His lips curved in an appreciative smile. His eyes traveled the length of her dress resting briefly on her cleavage before they set on her face. Was it her imagination or was he being flirtatious? She furrowed her brow. If she had any notion on how to reciprocate, she would go in for the kill. As it was, her talents never strayed in that direction. Besides, he was the dean of her department. Even so a warm glow crept up her thighs at his glance.

"Thank you." It wasn't her intention, but there was a small lift at the end of her statement like she'd asked a question. She wasn't going to belay that point and charged on. "My Uncle Harry is very proud of his collection."

"I bet he is," he said looking back at the paintings. "It is a very eclectic collection."

"I'll say." She favored him with her most dazzling smile.

He turned his back to her, hands clasped behind his back. It wasn't lost on her how that pose showed off the strength of his physique. A plane so smooth a woman could expertly trail a finger across it. She took a quick sip of her drink to stave off the wicked thought. He was the dean of the art school for crying out loud.

"You are quite talented." This time he didn't smile, and the air was somewhat colder for its absence.

"It's not my best work." Sophie swallowed.

"I can't argue with that." His eyes gleamed. "You really should paint a subject of your own. I'd be dying to see it."

"We'll see what the future holds." She pressed her lips together to keep the torrent of adoration escaping her mouth. He was just so breathtaking. It was a crime not to blurt it out. One thousand one…One thousand two…deep breath. "Well, I must return to my guests."

Sophie swiveled on her heels, but he caught her and turned her back to him. "What's wrong?"

He looked at her with such concern her heart nearly burst. She didn't know how to act around him anymore. Their discourse was much easier when they were pursuing Overton. Now it was as if they were naked with nothing between them but air. So she said the first thing that popped into her mind. "I haven't found a job. My parents are prepared to ship me off to London."

"Maybe I could help with that." He fished into his pocket grinning like a kid at Christmas. "I've put in a good word for you at the Boston Monitor. Here is their number." He handed her a slip of paper. "They're expecting a call on Monday."

"Oh." Sophie was stunned at how generous Raymond could be.

"The rest is up to you." He tapped her nose. "But I have faith in you."

"Thank you. You can't know what this means to me."

"If it keeps you in the Boston area that's in my interest."

"Why?" She stared up into his handsome face wondering how she ever could have found an imperfection. He took her hand.

"I think it's time we go on a proper date." Before she could utter a word, he drew her in for a kiss. His lips were warm and tender warming her soul with pride and happiness. She wrapped her arms around his neck returning his kiss. Her future no longer looked bleak but held the promise of adventure and fulfillment.

A word about the author...

Krysta Scott has always been a daydreamer, imagining worlds far away with happy endings. When she was in fifth grade, she was so caught up in fantasy she earned the dubious distinction of being named the girl who daydreams the most. The award for this questionable honor was a colorful transparent plastic poster made to look like stained glass. It was very cool. Given her flights of fancy, it came as no surprise to her family when she announced she was going to be an actress. Unfortunately, her pursuit into theater didn't last long because she was too withdrawn and shy to exhibit any talent in this area. Left with no other choice but to pursue a more practical avocation, she decided to major in psychology and then go to law school. Not able to let go of the worlds she created in her head, she returned to writing and was very excited when The Wild Rose Press contracted her first book.

Thank you for purchasing
this publication of The Wild Rose Press, Inc.

For questions or more information
contact us at
info@thewildrosepress.com.

The Wild Rose Press, Inc.
www.thewildrosepress.com